SECRET HISTORIES

Volume II of
The Purcell Papers

Other books by J. Sheridan LeFanu

SECRET HISTORIES

Volume II of
The Purcell Papers

J. Sheridan LeFanu

WILDSIDE PRESS
Doylestown, Pennsylvania

From the 1880 Richard Bentley and Son edition.

Secret Histories
A publication of
Wildside Press
P.O. Box 301
Holicong, PA 18928-0301

www.wildsidepress.com

Table of Contents

THE
PURCELL
PAPERS

Volume II

Passage in the Secret History of an Irish Countess

Being a Fifth Extract from the Legacy of the late Francis Purcell, P.P. of Drumcoolagh

*T*he following paper is written in a female hand, and was no doubt communicated to my much-regretted friend by the lady whose early history it serves to illustrate, the Countess D——. She is no more — she long since died, a childless and a widowed wife, and, as her letter sadly predicts, none survive to whom the publication of this narrative can prove "injurious, or even painful." Strange! two powerful and wealthy families, that in which she was born, and that into which she had married, have ceased to be — they are utterly extinct.

To those who know anything of the history of Irish families, as they were less than a century ago, the facts which immediately follow will at once suggest *the names* of the principal actors; and to others their publication would be useless — to us, possibly, if not probably, injurious. I have, therefore, altered such of the names as might, if stated, get us into difficulty; others, belonging to minor characters in the strange story, I have left untouched.

My Dear Friend, —
You have asked me to furnish you with a detail of the strange events which marked my early history, and I have, without hesitation, applied myself to the task, knowing that, while I live, a kind consideration for my feelings will prevent your giving publicity to the statement; and conscious that, when I am no more, there will not survive one to whom the narrative can prove injurious, or even painful.

My mother died when I was quite an infant, and of her I have no recollection, even the faintest. By her death, my education and habits were left solely to the guidance of my surviving parent; and, as far as a stern attention to my religious instruction, and an active anxiety evinced by his procuring for me the best masters to perfect me in those accomplishments which my station and wealth might seem to require, could avail, he amply discharged the task.

My father was what is called an oddity, and his treatment of me, though uniformly kind, flowed less from affection and tenderness than from a sense of obligation and duty. Indeed, I seldom even spoke to him except at meal-times, and then his manner was silent and abrupt; his leisure hours, which were many, were passed either in his study or in solitary walks; in short, he seemed to take no further interest in my happiness or improvement than a conscientious regard to the discharge of his own duty would seem to claim.

Shortly before my birth a circumstance had occurred which had contributed much to form and to confirm my father's secluded habits — it was the fact that a suspicion of *murder* had fallen upon his younger brother, though not sufficiently definite to lead to an indictment, yet strong enough to ruin him in public opinion.

This disgraceful and dreadful doubt cast upon the family name, my father felt deeply and bitterly, and not the less so that he himself was thoroughly convinced of his brother's innocence. The sincerity and strength of this impression he shortly afterwards proved in a manner which produced the dark events which follow. Before, however, I enter upon the statement of them, I ought to relate the circumstances which had awakened the suspicion; inasmuch as they are in themselves somewhat curious, and, in their effects, most intimately connected with my after-history.

My uncle, Sir Arthur T——n, was a gay and extravagant man, and, among other vices, was ruinously addicted to gaming; this unfortunate propensity, even after his fortune had suffered so severely as to render inevitable a reduction in his expenses by no means inconsiderable, nevertheless continued to actuate him, nearly to the exclusion of all other pursuits; he was, however, a proud, or rather a vain man, and could not bear to make the diminution of his income a matter of gratulation and triumph to those with whom he had hitherto competed, and the consequence was, that he frequented no longer the expensive haunts of dissipation, and retired from the gay world, leaving his coterie to discover his reasons as best they might.

He did not, however, forego his favorite vice, for,

though he could not worship his great divinity in the costly temples where it was formerly his wont to take his stand, yet he found it very possible to bring about him a sufficient number of the votaries of chance to answer all his ends. The consequence was, that Carrickleigh, which was the name of my uncle's residence, was never without one or more of such visitors as I have described.

It happened that upon one occasion he was visited by one Hugh Tisdall, a gentleman of loose habits, but of considerable wealth, and who had, in early youth, traveled with my uncle upon the Continent; the period of his visit was winter, and, consequently, the house was nearly deserted excepting by its regular inmates; it was therefore highly acceptable, particularly as my uncle was aware that his visitor's tastes accorded exactly with his own.

Both parties seemed determined to avail themselves of their suitability during the brief stay which Mr. Tisdall had promised; the consequence was, that they shut themselves up in Sir Arthur's private room for nearly all the day and the greater part of the night, during the space of nearly a week, at the end of which the servant having one morning, as usual, knocked at Mr. Tisdall's bedroom door repeatedly, received no answer, and, upon attempting to enter, found that it was locked; this appeared suspicious, and, the inmates of the house having been alarmed, the door was forced open, and, on proceeding to the bed, they found the body of its occupant perfectly lifeless, and hanging half-way out, the head downwards, and near the floor. One deep wound had been inflicted upon the temple, apparently with some blunt instrument which had penetrated the brain; and another blow, less effective, probably the first aimed, had grazed the head, removing some of the scalp, but leaving the skull untouched.

The door had been double-locked upon the *inside,* in evidence of which the key still lay where it had been placed in the lock.

The window, though not secured on the interior, was closed — a circumstance not a little puzzling, as it afforded the only other mode of escape from the room; it looked out, too, upon a kind of courtyard, round which the old buildings stood, formerly accessible by a narrow doorway and passage lying in the oldest side of the quadrangle, but which had since been built up, so as to preclude all ingress or egress; the room was also upon the second story, and the height of the window considerable. Near the bed were found a pair of razors belonging to the murdered man, one of them upon the ground, and both of them open. The weapon which had inflicted the mortal wound was not to be found in the room, nor were any footsteps or other traces of the murderer discoverable.

At the suggestion of Sir Arthur himself, a coroner was instantly summoned to attend, and an inquest was held; nothing, however, in any degree conclusive was elicited; the walls, ceiling, and floor of the room were carefully examined, in order to ascertain whether they contained a trapdoor or other concealed mode of entrance — but no such thing appeared.

Such was the minuteness of investigation employed, that, although the grate had contained a large fire during the night, they proceeded to examine even the very chimney, in order to discover whether escape by it were possible; but this attempt, too, was fruitless, for the chimney, built in the old fashion, rose in a perfectly perpendicular line from the hearth to a height of nearly fourteen feet above the roof, affording in its interior scarcely the possibility of ascent, the flue being smoothly plastered, and sloping towards the top like an inverted funnel, promising, too, even if the summit were attained, owing to its great height, but a precarious descent upon the sharp and steep-ridged roof; the ashes, too, which lay in the grate, and the soot, as far as it could be seen, were undisturbed, a circumstance almost conclusive of the question.

Sir Arthur was of course examined; his evidence was given with clearness and unreserve, which seemed calculated to silence all suspicion. He stated that, up to the day and night immediately preceding the catastrophe, he had lost to a heavy amount, but that, at their last sitting, he had not only won back his original loss, but upwards of four thousand pounds in addition; in evidence of which he produced an acknowledgment of debt to that amount in the handwriting of the deceased, and bearing the date of the fatal night. He had mentioned the circumstance to his lady, and in presence of some of the domestics; which statement was supported by *their* respective evidence.

One of the jury shrewdly observed, that the circumstance of Mr. Tisdall's having sustained so heavy a loss might have suggested to some ill-minded persons accidentally hearing it, the plan of robbing him, after having murdered him in such a manner as might make it appear that he had committed suicide; a supposition which was strongly supported by the razors having been found thus displaced, and removed from their case. Two persons had probably been engaged in the attempt, one watching by the sleeping man, and ready to strike him in case of his awakening suddenly, while the other was procuring the razors and employed in inflicting the fatal gash, so as to make it appear to have been the act of the murdered man himself. It was said that while the juror was making this suggestion Sir Arthur changed color.

Nothing, however, like legal evidence appeared against him, and the consequence was that the verdict was found against a person or persons unknown; and for some time the matter was suffered to rest, until, after about five months, my father received a letter from a person signing himself Andrew Collis, and representing himself to be the cousin of the deceased. This letter stated that Sir Arthur was likely to incur not merely suspicion, but personal risk, unless he could account for certain circumstances connected with the recent murder, and contained a copy of a letter written by the deceased, and bearing date, the day of the week, and of the month, upon the night of which the deed of blood had been perpetrated. Tisdall's note ran as follows:

"Dear Collis,

"I have had sharp work with Sir Arthur; he tried some of his stale tricks, but soon found that *I* was Yorkshire too: it would not do — you understand me. We went to the work like good ones, head, heart and soul; and, in fact, since I came here, I have lost no time. I am rather fagged, but I am sure to be well paid for my hardship; I never want sleep so long as I can have the music of a dice-box, and wherewithal to pay the piper. As I told you, he tried some of his queer turns, but I foiled him like a man, and, in return, gave him more than he could relish of the genuine *dead knowledge.*

"In short, I have plucked the old baronet as never baronet was plucked before; I have scarce left him the stump of a quill; I have got promissory notes in his hand to the amount of — if you like round numbers, say, thirty thousand pounds, safely deposited in my portable strongbox, alias double-clasped pocketbook. I leave this ruinous old rat-hole early on tomorrow, for two reasons — first, I do not want to play with Sir Arthur deeper than I think his security, that is, his money, or his money's worth, would warrant; and, secondly, because I am safer a hundred miles from Sir Arthur than in the house with him. Look you, my worthy, I tell you this between ourselves — I may be wrong, but, by G——, I am as sure as that I am now living, that Sir A—— attempted to poison me last night; so much for old friendship on both sides.

"When I won the last stake, a heavy one enough, my friend leant his forehead upon his hands, and you'll laugh when I tell you that his head literally smoked like a hot dumpling. I do not know whether his agitation was produced by the plan which he had against me, or by his having lost so heavily — though it must be allowed that he had reason to be a little funked, whichever way his thoughts went; but he pulled the bell, and ordered two bottles of champagne. While the fellow was bringing them he drew out a promissory note to the full amount, which he signed, and, as the man came in with the bottles and glasses, he desired him to be off; he filled out a glass for me, and, while he thought my eyes were off, for I was putting up his note at the time, he dropped something slyly into it, no doubt to sweeten it; but I saw it all, and, when he handed it to me, I said, with an emphasis which he might or might not understand:

"'There is some sediment in this; I'll not drink it.'

"'Is there?' said he, and at the same time snatched it from my hand and threw it into the fire. What do you think of that? have I not a tender chicken to manage? Win or lose, I will not play beyond five thousand tonight, and tomorrow sees me safe out of the reach of Sir Arthur's champagne. So, all things considered, I think you must allow that you are not the last who have found a knowing boy in

> "Yours to command,
> "HUGH TISDALL"

Of the authenticity of this document I never heard my father express a doubt; and I am satisfied that, owing to his strong conviction in favor of his brother, he would not have admitted it without sufficient inquiry, inasmuch as it tended to confirm the suspicions which already existed to his prejudice.

Now, the only point in this letter which made strongly against my uncle, was the mention of the "double-clasped pocketbook" as the receptacle of the papers likely to involve him, for this pocketbook was not forthcoming, nor anywhere to be found, nor had any papers referring to his gaming transactions been found upon the dead man. However, whatever might have been the original intention of this Collis, neither my uncle nor my father ever heard more of him; but he published the letter in Faulkner's newspaper, which was shortly afterwards made the vehicle of a much more mysterious attack. The passage in that periodical to which I allude, occurred about four years afterwards, and while the fatal occurrence was still fresh in public recollection. It commenced by a rambling preface, stating that "a *certain person* whom *certain* persons thought to be dead, was not so, but living, and in full possession of his memory, and moreover ready and able to make *great* delinquents tremble." It then went on to describe the murder, without, however, mentioning names; and in doing so, it entered into minute and circumstantial particulars of which none but an *eyewitness* could have been possessed, and by implications almost too unequivocal to be regarded in the light of insinuation, to involve the *"titled gambler"* in the guilt of the transaction.

My father at once urged Sir Arthur to proceed

against the paper in an action of libel; but he would not hear of it, nor consent to my father's taking any legal steps whatever in the matter. My father, however, wrote in a threatening tone to Faulkner, demanding a surrender of the author of the obnoxious article. The answer to this application is still in my possession, and is penned in an apologetic tone: it states that the manuscript had been handed in, paid for, and inserted as an advertisement, without sufficient inquiry, or any knowledge as to whom it referred.

No step, however, was taken to clear my uncle's character in the judgment of the public; and as he immediately sold a small property, the application of the proceeds of which was known to none, he was said to have disposed of it to enable himself to buy off the threatened information. However the truth might have been, it is certain that no charges respecting the mysterious murder were afterwards publicly made against my uncle, and, as far as external disturbances were concerned, he enjoyed henceforward perfect security and quiet.

A deep and lasting impression, however, had been made upon the public mind, and Sir Arthur T——n was no longer visited or noticed by the gentry and aristocracy of the county, whose attention and courtesies he had hitherto received. He accordingly affected to despise these enjoyments which he could not procure, and shunned even that society which he might have commanded.

This is all that I need recapitulate of my uncle's history, and I now recur to my own. Although my father had never, within my recollection, visited, or been visited by, my uncle, each being of sedentary, procrastinating, and secluded habits, and their respective residences being very far apart — the one lying in the county of Galway, the other in that of Cork — he was strongly attached to his brother, and evinced his affection by an active correspondence, and by deeply and proudly resenting that neglect which had marked Sir Arthur as unfit to mix in society.

When I was about eighteen years of age, my father, whose health had been gradually declining, died, leaving me in heart wretched and desolate, and, owing to his previous seclusion, with few acquaintances, and almost no friends.

The provisions of his will were curious, and when I had sufficiently come to myself to listen to or comprehend them, surprised me not a little: all his vast property was left to me, and to the heirs of my body, forever; and, in default of such heirs, it was to go after my death to my uncle, Sir Arthur, without any entail.

At the same time, the will appointed him my guardian, desiring that I might be received within his house, and reside with his family, and under his care, during the term of my minority; and in consideration of the increased expense consequent upon such an arrangement, a handsome annuity was allotted to him during the term of my proposed residence.

The object of this last provision I at once understood: my father desired, by making it the direct, apparent interest of Sir Arthur that I should die without issue, while at the same time he placed me wholly in his power, to prove to the world how great and unshaken was his confidence in his brother's innocence and honor, and also to afford him an opportunity of showing that this mark of confidence was not unworthily bestowed.

It was a strange, perhaps an idle scheme; but as I had been always brought up in the habit of considering my uncle as a deeply-injured man, and had been taught, almost as a part of my religion, to regard him as the very soul of honor, I felt no further uneasiness respecting the arrangement than that likely to result to a timid girl, of secluded habits, from the immediate prospect of taking up her abode for the first time in her life among total strangers. Previous to leaving my home, which I felt I should do with a heavy heart, I received a most tender and affectionate letter from my uncle, calculated, if anything could do so, to remove the bitterness of parting from scenes familiar and dear from my earliest childhood, and in some degree to reconcile me to the measure.

It was during a fine autumn that I approached the old domain of Carrickleigh. I shall not soon forget the impression of sadness and of gloom which all that I saw produced upon my mind; the sunbeams were falling with a rich and melancholy tint upon the fine old trees, which stood in lordly groups, casting their long, sweeping shadows over rock and sward. There was an air of neglect and decay about the spot, which amounted almost to desolation; the symptoms of this increased in number as we approached the building itself, near which the ground had been originally more artificially and carefully cultivated than elsewhere, and whose neglect consequently more immediately and strikingly betrayed itself.

As we proceeded, the road wound near the beds of what had been formerly two fish-ponds, which were now nothing more than stagnant swamps, overgrown with rank weeds, and here and there encroached upon by the straggling underwood; the avenue itself was much broken, and in many places the stones were almost concealed by grass and nettles; the loose stone walls which had here and there intersected the broad park were, in many places, broken down, so as no longer to answer their original purpose as fences; piers were now and then to be seen, but the gates were gone; and, to add to the general air of dilapidation, some huge trunks were lying scattered through the venerable old trees, either the work of the winter storms, or perhaps the victims of some extensive but desultory scheme of denudation, which the projector had not capital or perseverance to carry into full effect.

After the carriage had traveled a mile of this avenue, we reached the summit of rather an abrupt eminence, one of the many which added to the picturesqueness, if not to the convenience of this rude passage. From the top of this ridge the grey walls of Carrickleigh were visible, rising at a small distance in front, and darkened by the hoary wood which crowded around them. It was a quadrangular building of considerable extent, and the front which lay towards us, and in which the great entrance was placed, bore unequivocal marks of antiquity; the time-worn, solemn aspect of the old building, the ruinous and deserted appearance of the whole place, and the associations which connected it with a dark page in the history of my family, combined to depress spirits already predisposed for the reception of somber and dejecting impressions.

When the carriage drew up in the grass-grown courtyard before the hall-door, two lazy-looking men, whose appearance well accorded with that of the place which they tenanted, alarmed by the obstreperous barking of a great chained dog, ran out from some half-ruinous outhouses, and took charge of the horses; the hall-door stood open, and I entered a gloomy and imperfectly lighted apartment, and found no one within. However, I had not long to wait in this awkward predicament, for before my luggage had been deposited in the house, indeed, before I had well removed my cloak and other wraps, so as to enable me to look around, a young girl ran lightly into the hall, and kissing me heartily, and somewhat boisterously, exclaimed:

"My dear cousin, my dear Margaret — I am so delighted — so out of breath. We did not expect you till ten o'clock; my father is somewhere about the place, he must be close at hand. James — Corney — run out and tell your master — my brother is seldom at home, at least at any reasonable hour — you must be so tired — so fatigued — let me show you to your room — see that Lady Margaret's luggage is all brought up — you must lie down and rest yourself — Deborah, bring some coffee — up these stairs; we are so delighted to see you — you cannot think how lonely I have been — how steep these stairs are, are not they? I am so glad you are come — I could hardly bring myself to believe that you were really coming — how good of you, dear Lady Margaret."

There was real good-nature and delight in my cousin's greeting, and a kind of constitutional confidence of manner which placed me at once at ease, and made me feel immediately upon terms of intimacy with her. The room into which she ushered me, although partaking in the general air of decay which pervaded the mansion and all about it, had nevertheless been fitted up with evident attention to comfort, and even with some dingy attempt at luxury; but what pleased me most was that it opened, by a second door, upon a lobby which communicated with my fair cousin's apartment; a circumstance which divested the room, in my eyes, of the air of solitude and sadness which would otherwise have characterized it, to a degree almost painful to one so dejected in spirits as I was.

After such arrangements as I found necessary were completed, we both went down to the parlor, a large wainscoted room, hung round with grim old portraits, and, as I was not sorry to see, containing in its ample grate a large and cheerful fire. Here my cousin had leisure to talk more at her ease; and from her I learned something of the manners and the habits of the two remaining members of her family, whom I had not yet seen.

On my arrival I had known nothing of the family among whom I was come to reside, except that it consisted of three individuals, my uncle, and his son and daughter, Lady T——n having been long dead. In addition to this very scanty stock of information, I shortly learned from my communicative companion that my uncle was, as I had suspected, completely retired in his habits, and besides that, having been so far back as she could well recollect, always rather strict, as reformed rakes frequently become, he had latterly been growing more gloomily and sternly religious than heretofore.

Her account of her brother was far less favorable, though she did not say anything directly to his disadvantage. From all that I could gather from her, I was led to suppose that he was a specimen of the idle, coarse-mannered, profligate, low-minded *"squirearchy"* — a result which might naturally have flowed from the circumstance of his being, as it were, outlawed from society, and driven for companionship to grades below his own — enjoying, too, the dangerous prerogative of spending much money.

However, you may easily suppose that I found nothing in my cousin's communication fully to bear me out in so very decided a conclusion.

I awaited the arrival of my uncle, which was every moment to be expected, with feelings half of alarm, half of curiosity — a sensation which I have often since experienced, though to a less degree, when upon the point of standing for the first time in the presence of one of whom I have long been in the habit of hearing or thinking with interest.

It was, therefore, with some little perturbation that

I heard, first a slight bustle at the outer door, then a slow step traverse the hall, and finally witnessed the door open, and my uncle enter the room. He was a striking-looking man; from peculiarities both of person and of garb, the whole effect of his appearance amounted to extreme singularity. He was tall, and when young his figure must have been strikingly elegant; as it was, however, its effect was marred by a very decided stoop. His dress was of a sober color, and in fashion anterior to anything which I could remember. It was, however, handsome, and by no means carelessly put on; but what completed the singularity of his appearance was his uncut, white hair, which hung in long, but not at all neglected curls, even so far as his shoulders, and which combined with his regularly classic features, and fine dark eyes, to bestow upon him an air of venerable dignity and pride, which I have never seen equaled elsewhere. I rose as he entered, and met him about the middle of the room; he kissed my cheek and both my hands, saying:

"You are most welcome, dear child, as welcome as the command of this poor place and all that it contains can make you. I am most rejoiced to see you — truly rejoiced. I trust that you are not much fatigued — pray be seated again." He led me to my chair, and continued: "I am glad to perceive you have made acquaintance with Emily already; I see, in your being thus brought together, the foundation of a lasting friendship. You are both innocent, and both young. God bless you — God bless you, and make you all that I could wish."

He raised his eyes, and remained for a few moments silent, as if in secret prayer. I felt that it was impossible that this man, with feelings so quick, so warm, so tender, could be the wretch that public opinion had represented him to be. I was more than ever convinced of his innocence.

His manner was, or appeared to me, most fascinating; there was a mingled kindness and courtesy in it which seemed to speak benevolence itself. It was a manner which I felt cold art could never have taught; it owed most of its charm to its appearing to emanate directly from the heart; it must be a genuine index of the owner's mind. So I thought.

My uncle having given me fully to understand that I was most welcome, and might command whatever was his own, pressed me to take some refreshment; and on my refusing, he observed that previously to bidding me good-night, he had one duty further to perform, one in whose observance he was convinced I would cheerfully acquiesce.

He then proceeded to read a chapter from the Bible; after which he took his leave with the same affectionate kindness with which he had greeted me, having repeated his desire that I should consider everything in his house as altogether at my disposal. It is needless to say that I was much pleased with my uncle — it was impossible to avoid being so; and I could not help saying to myself, if such a man as this is not safe from the assaults of slander, who is? I felt much happier than I had done since my father's death, and enjoyed that night the first refreshing sleep which had visited me since that event.

My curiosity respecting my male cousin did not long remain unsatisfied — he appeared the next day at dinner. His manners, though not so coarse as I had expected, were exceedingly disagreeable; there was an assurance and a forwardness for which I was not prepared; there was less of the vulgarity of manner, and almost more of that of the mind, than I had anticipated. I felt quite uncomfortable in his presence; there was just that confidence in his look and tone which would read encouragement even in mere toleration; and I felt more disgusted and annoyed at the coarse and extravagant compliments which he was pleased from time to time to pay me, than perhaps the extent of the atrocity might fully have warranted. It was, however, one consolation that he did not often appear, being much engrossed by pursuits about which I neither knew nor cared anything; but when he did appear, his attentions, either with a view to his amusement or to some more serious advantage, were so obviously and perseveringly directed to me, that young and inexperienced as I was, even *I* could not be ignorant of his preference. I felt more provoked by this odious persecution than I can express, and discouraged him with so much vigor, that I employed even rudeness to convince him that his assiduities were unwelcome; but all in vain.

This had gone on for nearly a twelve-month, to my infinite annoyance, when one day as I was sitting at some needle-work with my companion Emily, as was my habit, in the parlor, the door opened, and my cousin Edward entered the room. There was something, I thought, odd in his manner — a kind of struggle between shame and impudence — a kind of flurry and ambiguity which made him appear, if possible, more than ordinarily disagreeable.

"Your servant, ladies," he said, seating himself at the same time; "sorry to spoil your *tête-à-tête*, but never mind, I'll only take Emily's place for a minute or two; and then we part for a while, fair cousin. Emily, my father wants you in the corner turret. No shilly-shally; he's in a hurry." She hesitated. "Be off — tramp, march!" he exclaimed, in a tone which the poor girl dared not disobey.

She left the room, and Edward followed her to the door. He stood there for a minute or two, as if reflecting what he should say, perhaps satisfying himself that no one was within hearing in the hall.

At length he turned about, having closed the door, as if carelessly, with his foot; and advancing slowly, as if in deep thought, he took his seat at the side of the table opposite to mine.

There was a brief interval of silence, after which he said:

"I imagine that you have a shrewd suspicion of the object of my early visit; but I suppose I must go into particulars. Must I?"

"I have no conception," I replied, "what your object may be."

"Well, well," said he, becoming more at his ease as he proceeded, "it may be told in a few words. You know that it is totally impossible — quite out of the question — that an offhand young fellow like me, and a good-looking girl like yourself, could meet continually, as you and I have done, without an attachment — a liking growing up on one side or other; in short, I think I have let you know as plain as if I spoke it, that I have been in love with you almost from the first time I saw you."

He paused; but I was too much horrified to speak. He interpreted my silence favorably.

"I can tell you," he continued, "I'm reckoned rather hard to please, and very hard to *hit*. I can't say when I was taken with a girl before; so you see fortune reserved me —"

Here the odious wretch wound his arm round my waist. The action at once restored me to utterance, and with the most indignant vehemence I released myself from his hold, and at the same time said:

"I have not been insensible, sir, of your most disagreeable attentions — they have long been a source of much annoyance to me; and you must be aware that I have marked my disapprobation — my disgust — as unequivocally as I possibly could, without actual indelicacy."

I paused, almost out of breath from the rapidity with which I had spoken; and without giving him time to renew the conversation, I hastily quitted the room, leaving him in a paroxysm of rage and mortification. As I ascended the stairs, I heard him open the hall-door with violence, and take two or three rapid strides in the direction in which I was moving. I was now much frightened, and ran the whole way until I reached my room; and having locked the door, I listened breathlessly, but heard no sound. This relieved me for the present; but so much had I been overcome by the agitation and annoyance attendant upon the scene which I had just gone through, that when my cousin Emily knocked at my door, I was weeping in strong hysterics.

You will readily conceive my distress, when you reflect upon my strong dislike to my cousin Edward, combined with my youth and extreme inexperience. Any proposal of such a nature must have agitated me; but that it should have come from the man whom of all others I most loathed and abhorred, and to whom I had, as clearly as manner could do it, expressed the state of my feelings, was almost too overwhelming to be borne. It was a calamity, too, in which I could not claim the sympathy of my cousin Emily, which had always been extended to me in my minor grievances. Still I hoped that it might not be unattended with good; for I thought that one inevitable and most welcome consequence would result from this painful *eclaircissment,* in the discontinuance of my cousin's odious persecution.

When I arose next morning, it was with the fervent hope that I might never again behold the face, or even hear the name, of my cousin Edward; but such a consummation, though devoutly to be wished, was hardly likely to occur. The painful impressions of yesterday were too vivid to be at once erased; and I could not help feeling some dim foreboding of coming annoyance and evil.

To expect on my cousin's part anything like delicacy or consideration for me, was out of the question. I saw that he had set his heart upon my property, and that he was not likely easily to forego such an acquisition — possessing what might have been considered opportunities and facilities almost to compel my compliance.

I now keenly felt the unreasonableness of my father's conduct in placing me to reside with a family of all whose members, with one exception, he was wholly ignorant, and I bitterly felt the helplessness of my situation. I determined, however, in case of my cousin's persevering in his addresses, to lay all the particulars before my uncle, although he had never in kindness or intimacy gone a step beyond our first interview, and to throw myself upon his hospitality and his sense of honor for protection against a repetition of such scenes.

My cousin's conduct may appear to have been an inadequate cause for such serious uneasiness; but my alarm was caused neither by his acts nor words, but entirely by his manner, which was strange and even intimidating to excess. At the beginning of the yesterday's interview there was a sort of bullying swagger in his air, which towards the end gave place to the brutal vehemence of an undisguised ruffian — a transition which had tempted me into a belief that he might seek even forcibly to extort from me a consent to his wishes, or by means still more horrible, of which I scarcely dared to trust myself to think, to possess himself of my property.

I was early next day summoned to attend my uncle in his private room, which lay in a corner turret of the old building; and thither I accordingly went, wondering all the way what this unusual measure might prelude. When I entered the room, he did not rise in his usual courteous way to greet me, but simply pointed to a chair opposite to his own. This boded nothing agreeable. I sat down, however, silently waiting until he should open the conversation.

"Lady Margaret," at length he said, in a tone of greater sternness than I thought him capable of using, "I have hitherto spoken to you as a friend, but I have not forgotten that I am also your guardian, and that my authority as such gives me a right to control your conduct. I shall put a question to you, and I expect and will demand a plain, direct answer. Have I rightly been informed that you have contemptuously rejected the suit and hand of my son Edward?"

I stammered forth with a good deal of trepidation:

"I believe — that is, I have, sir, rejected my cousin's proposals; and my coldness and discouragement might have convinced him that I had determined to do so."

"Madam," replied he, with suppressed, but, as it appeared to me, intense anger, "I have lived long enough to know that *coldness* and discouragement, and such terms, form the common cant of a worthless coquette. You know to the full, as well as I, that *coldness and discouragement* may be so exhibited as to convince their object that he is neither distasteful or indifferent to the person who wears this manner. You know, too, none better, that an affected neglect, when skillfully managed, is amongst the most formidable of the engines which artful beauty can employ. I tell you, madam, that having, without one word spoken in discouragement, permitted my son's most marked attentions for a twelvemonth or more, you have no right to dismiss him with no further explanation than demurely telling him that you had always looked coldly upon him; and neither your wealth nor your *ladyship*" (there was an emphasis of scorn on the word, which would have become Sir Giles Overreach himself) "can warrant you in treating with contempt the affectionate regard of an honest heart."

I was too much shocked at this undisguised attempt to bully me into an acquiescence in the interested and unprincipled plan for their own aggrandizement, which I now perceived my uncle and his son to have deliberately entered into, at once to find strength or collectedness to frame an answer to what he had said. At length I replied, with some firmness:

"In all that you have just now said, sir, you have grossly misstated my conduct and motives. Your information must have been most incorrect as far as it regards my conduct towards my cousin; my manner towards him could have conveyed nothing but dislike; and if anything could have added to the strong aversion which I have long felt towards him, it would be his attempting thus to trick and frighten me into a marriage which he knows to be revolting to me, and which is sought by him only as a means for securing to himself whatever property is mine."

As I said this, I fixed my eyes upon those of my uncle, but he was too old in the world's ways to falter beneath the gaze of more searching eyes than mine; he simply said:

"Are you acquainted with the provisions of your father's will?"

I answered in the affirmative; and he continued:

"Then you must be aware that if my son Edward were — which God forbid — the unprincipled, reckless man you pretend to think him" — (here he spoke very slowly, as if he intended that every word which escaped him should be registered in my memory, while at the same time the expression of his countenance underwent a gradual but horrible change, and the eyes which he fixed upon me became so darkly vivid, that I almost lost sight of everything else) — "if he were what you have described him, think you, girl, he could find no briefer means than wedding contracts to gain his ends? 'twas but to gripe your slender neck until the breath had stopped, and lands, and lakes, and all were his."

I stood staring at him for many minutes after he had ceased to speak, fascinated by the terrible serpent-like gaze, until he continued with a welcome change of countenance:

"I will not speak again to you upon this — topic until one month has passed. You shall have time to consider the relative advantages of the two courses which are open to you. I should be sorry to hurry you to a decision. I am satisfied with having stated my feelings upon the subject, and pointed out to you the path of duty. Remember this day month — not one word sooner."

He then rose, and I left the room, much agitated and exhausted.

This interview, all the circumstances attending it, but most particularly the formidable expression of my uncle's countenance while he talked, though hypothetically, of murder, combined to arouse all my worst suspicions of him. I dreaded to look upon the face that had so recently worn the appalling livery of guilt and malignity. I regarded it with the mingled fear and loathing with which one looks upon an object which has tortured them in a nightmare.

In a few days after the interview, the particulars of which I have just related, I found a note upon my toilet-table, and on opening it I read as follows:

"My Dear Lady Margaret,
"You will be perhaps surprised to see a strange face in your room today. I have dismissed your Irish maid, and secured a French one to wait upon you — a step rendered necessary by my proposing shortly to visit the Continent, with all my family.
"Your faithful guardian,
"Arthur T——n."

On inquiry, I found that my faithful attendant was actually gone, and far on her way to the town of Galway; and in her stead there appeared a tall, raw-boned, ill-looking, elderly Frenchwoman, whose sullen and presuming manners seemed to imply that her vocation had never before been that of a lady's-maid. I could not help regarding her as a creature of my uncle's, and therefore to be dreaded, even had she been in no other way suspicious.

Days and weeks passed away without any, even a momentary doubt upon my part, as to the course to be pursued by me. The allotted period had at length elapsed; the day arrived on which I was to communicate my decision to my uncle. Although my resolution had never for a moment wavered, I could not shake of the dread of the approaching colloquy; and my heart sunk within me as I heard the expected summons.

I had not seen my cousin Edward since the occurrence of the grand *eclaircissment*; he must have studiously avoided me — I suppose from policy, it could not have been from delicacy. I was prepared for a terrific burst of fury from my uncle, as soon as I should make known my determination; and I not unreasonably feared that some act of violence or of intimidation would next be resorted to.

Filled with these dreary forebodings, I fearfully opened the study door, and the next minute I stood

in my uncle's presence. He received me with a politeness which I dreaded, as arguing a favorable anticipation respecting the answer which I was to give; and
after some slight delay, he began by saying:

"It will be a relief to both of us, I believe, to bring
this conversation as soon as possible to an issue. You
will excuse me, then, my dear niece, for speaking with
an abruptness which, under other circumstances,
would be unpardonable. You have, I am certain, given
the subject of our last interview fair and serious consideration; and I trust that you are now prepared with
candor to lay your answer before me. A few words will
suffice — we perfectly understand one another."

He paused, and I, though feeling that I stood upon
a mine which might in an instant explode, nevertheless
answered with perfect composure:

"I must now, sir, make the same reply which I did
upon the last occasion, and I reiterate the declaration
which I then made, that I never can nor will, while life
and reason remain, consent to a union with my cousin
Edward."

This announcement wrought no apparent change in
Sir Arthur, except that he became deadly, almost lividly
pale. He seemed lost in dark thought for a minute, and
then with a slight effort said:

"You have answered me honestly and directly; and
you say your resolution is unchangeable. Well, would
it had been otherwise — would it had been otherwise
— but be it as it is — I am satisfied."

He gave me his hand — it was cold and damp as
death; under an assumed calmness, it was evident that
he was fearfully agitated. He continued to hold my
hand with an almost painful pressure, while, as if
unconsciously, seeming to forget my presence, he mut-
tered:

"Strange, strange, strange, indeed! fatuity, helpless

fatuity!" there was here a long pause. "Madness *indeed* to strain a cable that is rotten to the very heart — it must break — and then — all goes."

There was again a pause of some minutes, after which, suddenly changing his voice and manner to one of wakeful alacrity, he exclaimed:

"Margaret, my son Edward shall plague you no more. He leaves this country on tomorrow for France — he shall speak no more upon this subject — never, never more — whatever events depended upon your answer must now take their own course; but, as for this fruitless proposal, it has been tried enough; it can be repeated no more."

At these words he coldly suffered my hand to drop, as if to express his total abandonment of all his projected schemes of alliance; and certainly the action, with the accompanying words, produced upon my mind a more solemn and depressing effect than I believed possible to have been caused by the course which I had determined to pursue; it struck upon my heart with an awe and heaviness which *will* accompany the accomplishment of an important and irrevocable act, even though no doubt or scruple remains to make it possible that the agent should wish it undone.

"Well," said my uncle, after a little time, "we now cease to speak upon this topic, never to resume it again. Remember you shall have no farther uneasiness from Edward; he leaves Ireland for France on tomorrow; this will be a relief to you. May I depend upon your *honor* that no word touching the subject of this interview shall ever escape you?"

I gave him the desired assurance; he said:

"It is well — I am satisfied — we have nothing more, I believe, to say upon either side, and my presence must be a restraint upon you, I shall therefore bid you farewell."

I then left the apartment, scarcely knowing what to think of the strange interview which had just taken place.

On the next day my uncle took occasion to tell me that Edward had actually sailed, if his intention had not been interfered with by adverse circumstances; and two days subsequently he actually produced a letter from his son, written, as it said, *on board,* and dispatched while the ship was getting under weigh. This was a great satisfaction to me, and as being likely to prove so, it was no doubt communicated to me by Sir Arthur.

During all this trying period, I had found infinite consolation in the society and sympathy of my dear cousin Emily. I never in afterlife formed a friendship so close, so fervent, and upon which, in all its progress, I could look back with feelings of such unalloyed pleasure, upon whose termination I must ever dwell with so deep, yet so unembittered regret. In cheerful converse with her I soon recovered my spirits considerably, and passed my time agreeably enough, although still in the strictest seclusion.

Matters went on sufficiently smooth, although I could not help sometimes feeling a momentary, but horrible uncertainty respecting my uncle's character; which was not altogether unwarranted by the circumstances of the two trying interviews whose particulars I have just detailed. The unpleasant impression which these conferences were calculated to leave upon my mind, was fast wearing away, when there occurred a circumstance, slight indeed in itself, but calculated irresistibly to awaken all my worst suspicions, and to overwhelm me again with anxiety and terror.

I had one day left the house with my cousin Emily, in order to take a ramble of considerable length, for the purpose of sketching some favorite views, and we

had walked about half a mile when I perceived that we
had forgotten our drawing materials, the absence of
which would have defeated the object of our walk.
Laughing at our own thoughtlessness, we returned to
the house, and leaving Emily without, I ran upstairs
to procure the drawing-books and pencils, which lay
in my bedroom.

As I ran up the stairs I was met by the tall, ill-looking
Frenchwoman, evidently a good deal flurried.

"Que veut, Madame?" said she, with a more decided
effort to be polite than I had ever known her make
before.

"No, no — no matter," said I, hastily running by her
in the direction of my room.

"Madame," cried she, in a high key, "restez ici, s'il
vous plait; votre chambre n'est pas faite — your room
is not ready for your reception yet."

I continued to move on without heeding her. She
was some way behind me, and feeling that she could
not otherwise prevent my entrance, for I was now upon
the very lobby, she made a desperate attempt to seize
hold of my person: she succeeded in grasping the end
of my shawl, which she drew from my shoulders; but
slipping at the same time upon the polished oak floor,
she fell at full length upon the boards.

A little frightened as well as angry at the rudeness of
this strange woman, I hastily pushed open the door of
my room, at which I now stood, in order to escape
from her; but great was my amazement on entering to
find the apartment preoccupied.

The window was open, and beside it stood two male
figures; they appeared to be examining the fastenings
of the casement, and their backs were turned towards
the door. One of them was my uncle; they both turned
on my entrance, as if startled. The stranger was booted
and cloaked, and wore a heavy broad-leafed hat over

his brows. He turned but for a moment, and averted his face; but I had seen enough to convince me that he was no other than my cousin Edward. My uncle had some iron instrument in his hand, which he hastily concealed behind his back; and coming towards me, said something as if in an explanatory tone; but I was too much shocked and confounded to understand what it might be. He said something about *"repairs —* window — frames — cold, and safety."

I did not wait, however, to ask or to receive explanations, but hastily left the room. As I went down the stairs I thought I heard the voice of the Frenchwoman in all the shrill volubility of excuse, which was met, however, by suppressed but vehement imprecations, or what seemed to me to be such, in which the voice of my cousin Edward distinctly mingled.

I joined my cousin Emily quite out of breath. I need not say that my head was too full of other things to think much of drawing for that day. I imparted to her frankly the cause of my alarms, but at the same time as gently as I could; and with tears she promised vigilance, and devotion, and love. I never had reason for a moment to repent the unreserved confidence which I then reposed in her. She was no less surprised than I at the unexpected appearance of Edward, whose departure for France neither of us had for a moment doubted, but which was now proved by his actual presence to be nothing more than an imposture, practiced, I feared, for no good end.

The situation in which I had found my uncle had removed completely all my doubts as to his designs. I magnified suspicions into certainties, and dreaded night after night that I should be murdered in my bed. The nervousness produced by sleepless nights and days of anxious fears increased the horrors of my situation to such a degree, that I at length wrote a letter to a Mr.

Jefferies, an old and faithful friend of my father's, and perfectly acquainted with all his affairs, praying him, for God's sake, to relieve me from my present terrible situation, and communicating without reserve the nature and grounds of my suspicions.

This letter I kept sealed and directed for two or three days always about my person, for discovery would have been ruinous, in expectation of an opportunity which might be safely trusted, whereby to have it placed in the post office. As neither Emily nor I were permitted to pass beyond the precincts of the demesne itself, which was surrounded by high walls formed of dry stone, the difficulty of procuring such an opportunity was greatly enhanced.

At this time Emily had a short conversation with her father, which she reported to me instantly.

After some indifferent matter, he had asked her whether she and I were upon good terms, and whether I was unreserved in my disposition. She answered in the affirmative; and he then inquired whether I had been much surprised to find him in my chamber on the other day. She answered that I had been both surprised and amused.

"And what did she think of George Wilson's appearance?"

"Who?" inquired she.

"Oh, the architect," he answered, "who is to contract for the repairs of the house; he is accounted a handsome fellow."

"She could not see his face," said Emily, "and she was in such a hurry to escape that she scarcely noticed him."

Sir Arthur appeared satisfied, and the conversation ended.

This slight conversation, repeated accurately to me by Emily, had the effect of confirming, if indeed anything was required to do so, all that I had before believed as to Edward's actual presence; and I naturally became, if possible, more anxious than ever to dispatch the letter to Mr. Jefferies. An opportunity at length occurred.

As Emily and I were walking one day near the gate of the demesne, a lad from the village happened to be passing down the avenue from the house; the spot was secluded, and as this person was not connected by service with those whose observation I dreaded, I committed the letter to his keeping, with strict injunctions that he should put it without delay into the receiver of the town post office; at the same time I added a suitable gratuity, and the man having made many protestations of punctuality, was soon out of sight.

He was hardly gone when I began to doubt my discretion in having trusted this person; but I had no better or safer means of dispatching the letter, and I was not warranted in suspecting him of such wanton dishonesty as an inclination to tamper with it; but I could not be quite satisfied of its safety until I had received an answer, which could not arrive for a few days. Before I did, however, an event occurred which a little surprised me.

I was sitting in my bedroom early in the day, reading by myself, when I heard a knock at the door.

"Come in," said I; and my uncle entered the room.

"Will you excuse me?" said he. "I sought you in the parlor, and thence I have come here. I desired to say a word with you. I trust that you have hitherto found my conduct to you such as that of a guardian towards his ward should be."

I dared not withhold my consent.

"And," he continued, "I trust that you have not found me harsh or unjust, and that you have perceived, my dear niece, that I have sought to make this poor place as agreeable to you as may be."

I assented again; and he put his hand in his pocket, whence he drew a folded paper, and dashing it upon the table with startling emphasis, he said:

"Did you write that letter?"

The sudden and tearful alteration of his voice, manner, and face, but, more than all, the unexpected production of my letter to Mr. Jefferies, which I at once recognized, so confounded and terrified me, that I felt almost choking.

I could not utter a word.

"Did you write that letter?" he repeated with slow and intense emphasis."You did, liar and hypocrite! You dared to write this foul and infamous libel; but it shall be your last. Men will universally believe you mad, if I choose to call for an inquiry. I can make you appear so. The suspicions expressed in this letter are the hallucinations and alarms of moping lunacy. I have defeated your first attempt, madam; and by the holy God, if ever you make another, chains, straw, darkness, and the keeper's whip shall be your lasting portion!"

With these astounding words he left the room, leaving me almost fainting.

I was now almost reduced to despair; my last cast had failed; I had no course left but that of eloping secretly from the castle, and placing myself under the protection of the nearest magistrate. I felt if this were not done, and speedily, that I should be *murdered*.

No one, from mere description, can have an idea of the unmitigated horror of my situation — a helpless, weak, inexperienced girl, placed under the power and wholly at the mercy of evil men, and feeling that she had it not in her power to escape for a moment from the malignant influences under which she was probably fated to fall; and with a consciousness that if violence, if murder were designed, her dying shriek would be lost in void space; no human being would be near to aid her, no human interposition could deliver her.

I had seen Edward but once during his visit, and as I did not meet with him again, I began to think that he must have taken his departure — a conviction which was to a certain degree satisfactory, as I regarded his absence as indicating the removal of immediate danger.

Emily also arrived circuitously at the same conclusion, and not without good grounds, for she managed indirectly to learn that Edward's black horse had actually been for a day and part of a night in the castle stables, just at the time of her brother's supposed visit. The horse had gone, and, as she argued, the rider must have departed with it.

This point being so far settled, I felt a little less uncomfortable: when being one day alone in my bedroom, I happened to look out from the window, and, to my unutterable horror, I beheld, peering through an opposite casement, my cousin Edward's face. Had I seen the evil one himself in bodily shape, I could not have experienced a more sickening revulsion.

I was too much appalled to move at once from the window, but I did so soon enough to avoid his eye. He was looking fixedly into the narrow quadrangle upon which the window opened. I shrank back unperceived, to pass the rest of the day in terror and despair. I went to my room early that night, but I was too miserable to sleep.

At about twelve o'clock, feeling very nervous, I determined to call my cousin Emily, who slept, you will remember, in the next room, which communicated with mine by a second door. By this private entrance I found my way into her chamber, and without difficulty persuaded her to return to my room and sleep with me. We accordingly lay down together, she undressed, and I with my clothes on, for I was every moment walking up and down the room, and felt too nervous and miserable to think of rest or comfort.

Emily was soon fast asleep, and I lay awake, fervently longing for the first pale gleam of morning, reckoning every stroke of the old clock with an impatience which made every hour appear like six.

It must have been about one o'clock when I thought I heard a slight noise at the partition-door between Emily's room and mine, as if caused by somebody's turning the key in the lock. I held my breath, and the same sound was repeated at the second door of my room — that which opened upon the lobby — the sound was here distinctly caused by the revolution of the bolt in the lock, and it was followed by a slight pressure upon the door itself, as if to ascertain the security of the lock.

The person, whoever it might be, was probably satisfied, for I heard the old boards of the lobby creak and strain, as if under the weight of somebody moving cautiously over them. My sense of hearing became unnaturally, almost painfully acute. I suppose the imagination added distinctness to sounds vague in themselves. I thought that I could actually hear the breathing of the person who was slowly returning down the lobby. At the head of the staircase there appeared to occur a pause; and I could distinctly hear two or three sentences hastily whispered; the steps then descended the stairs with apparently less caution. I now ventured to walk quickly and lightly to the lobby-door, and attempted to open it; it was indeed fast locked upon the outside, as was also the other.

I now felt that the dreadful hour was come; but one desperate expedient remained — it was to awaken Emily, and by our united strength to attempt to force the partition-door, which was slighter than the other, and through this to pass to the lower part of the house, whence it might be possible to escape to the grounds, and forth to the village.

I returned to the bedside and shook Emily, but in vain. Nothing that I could do availed to produce from her more than a few incoherent words — it was a death-like sleep. She had certainly drank of some narcotic, as had I probably also, spite of all the caution with which I had examined everything presented to us to eat or drink.

I now attempted, with as little noise as possible, to force first one door, then the other — but all in vain. I believe no strength could have effected my object, for both doors opened inwards. I therefore collected whatever movables I could carry thither, and piled them against the doors, so as to assist me in whatever attempts I should make to resist the entrance of those without. I then returned to the bed and endeavored again, but fruitlessly, to awaken my cousin. It was not sleep, it was torpor, lethargy, death. I knelt down and prayed with an agony of earnestness; and then seating myself upon the bed, I awaited my fate with a kind of terrible tranquility.

I heard a faint clanking sound from the narrow court which I have already mentioned, as if caused by the scraping of some iron instrument against stones or rubbish. I at first determined not to disturb the calmness which I now felt, by uselessly watching the proceedings of those who sought my life; but as the sounds continued, the horrible curiosity which I felt overcame every other emotion, and I determined, at all hazards, to gratify it. I therefore crawled upon my knees to the window, so as to let the smallest portion of my head appear above the sill.

The moon was shining with an uncertain radiance

upon the antique grey buildings, and obliquely upon the narrow court beneath, one side of which was therefore clearly illuminated, while the other was lost in obscurity, the sharp outlines of the old gables, with their nodding clusters of ivy, being at first alone visible.

Whoever or whatever occasioned the noise which had excited my curiosity, was concealed under the shadow of the dark side of the quadrangle. I placed my hand over my eyes to shade them from the moonlight, which was so bright as to be almost dazzling, and, peering into the darkness, I first dimly, but afterwards gradually, almost with full distinctness, beheld the form of a man engaged in digging what appeared to be a rude hole close under the wall. Some implements, probably a shovel and pickaxe, lay beside him, and to these he every now and then applied himself as the nature of the ground required. He pursued his task rapidly, and with as little noise as possible.

"So," thought I, as, shovelful after shovelful, the dislodged rubbish mounted into a heap, "they are digging the grave in which, before two hours pass, I must lie, a cold, mangled corpse. I am *theirs* — I cannot escape."

I felt as if my reason was leaving me. I started to my feet, and in mere despair I applied myself again to each of the two doors alternately. I strained every nerve and sinew, but I might as well have attempted, with my single strength, to force the building itself from its foundation. I threw myself madly upon the ground, and clasped my hands over my eyes as if to shut out the horrible images which crowded upon me.

The paroxysm passed away. I prayed once more, with the bitter, agonized fervor of one who feels that the hour of death is present and inevitable. When I arose, I went once more to the window and looked out, just in time to see a shadowy figure glide stealthily along the wall. The task was finished. The catastrophe of the tragedy must soon be accomplished.

I determined now to defend my life to the last; and that I might be able to do so with some effect, I searched the room for something which might serve as a weapon; but either through accident, or from an anticipation of such a possibility, everything which might have been made available for such a purpose had been carefully removed. I must then die tamely and without an effort to defend myself.

A thought suddenly struck me — might it not be possible to escape through the door, which the assassin must open in order to enter the room? I resolved to make the attempt. I felt assured that the door through which ingress to the room would be effected, was that which opened upon the lobby. It was the more direct way, besides being, for obvious reasons, less liable to interruption than the other. I resolved, then, to place myself behind a projection of the wall, whose shadow would serve fully to conceal me, and when the door should be opened, and before they should have discovered the identity of the occupant of the bed, to creep noiselessly from the room, and then to trust to Providence for escape.

In order to facilitate this scheme, I removed all the lumber which I had heaped against the door; and I had nearly completed my arrangements, when I perceived the room suddenly darkened by the close approach of some shadowy object to the window. On turning my eyes in that direction, I observed at the top of the casement, as if suspended from above, first the feet, then the legs, then the body, and at length the whole figure of a man present himself. It was Edward T——n.

He appeared to be guiding his descent so as to bring his feet upon the center of the stone block which occupied the lower part of the window; and, having secured his footing upon this, he kneeled down and began to gaze into the room. As the moon was gleaming into the chamber, and the bed-curtains were drawn, he was able to distinguish the bed itself and its contents. He appeared satisfied with his scrutiny, for he looked up and made a sign with his hand, upon which the rope by which his descent had been effected was slackened from above, and he proceeded to disengage it from his waist; this accomplished, he applied his hands to the window-frame, which must have been ingeniously contrived for the purpose, for, with apparently no resistance, the whole frame, containing casement and all, slipped from its position in the wall, and was by him lowered into the room.

The cold night wind waved the bed-curtains, and he paused for a moment — all was still again — and he stepped in upon the floor of the room. He held in his hand what appeared to be a steel instrument, shaped something like a hammer, but larger and sharper at the extremities. This he held rather behind him, while, with three long, tip-toe strides, he brought himself to the bedside.

I felt that the discovery must now be made, and held my breath in momentary expectation of the execration in which he would vent his surprise and disappointment. I closed my eyes — there was a pause, but it was a short one. I heard two dull blows, given in rapid succession: a quivering sigh, and the long-drawn, heavy breathing of the sleeper was forever suspended. I unclosed my eyes, and saw the murderer fling the quilt across the head of his victim: he then, with the instrument of death still in his hand, proceeded to the lobby-door, upon which he tapped sharply twice or thrice. A quick step was then heard approaching, and a voice whispered something from without. Edward answered, with a kind of chuckle, "Her ladyship is past complaining; unlock the door, in the devil's name, unless you're afraid to come in, and help me to lift the body out of the window."

The key was turned in the lock — the door opened — and my uncle entered the room.

I have told you already that I had placed myself under the shade of a projection of the wall, close to the door. I had instinctively shrunk down, cowering towards the ground on the entrance of Edward through the window. When my uncle entered the room he and his son both stood so very close to me that his hand was every moment upon the point of touching my face. I held my breath, and remained motionless as death.

"You had no interruption from the next room?" said my uncle.

"No," was the brief reply.

"Secure the jewels, Ned; the French harpy must not lay her claws upon them. You're a steady hand, by G——! not much blood — eh?"

"Not twenty drops," replied his son, "and those on the quilt."

"I'm glad it's over," whispered my uncle again. "We must lift the — the *thing* through the window, and lay the rubbish over it."

They then turned to the bedside, and, winding the bed-clothes round the body, carried it between them slowly to the window, and, exchanging a few brief words with some one below, they shoved it over the windowsill, and I heard it fall heavily on the ground underneath.

"I'll take the jewels," said my uncle; "there are two caskets in the lower drawer."

He proceeded, with an accuracy which, had I been more at ease, would have furnished me with matter of astonishment, to lay his hand upon the very spot where my jewels lay; and having possessed himself of them, he called to his son:

"Is the rope made fast above?"

"I'm not a fool — to be sure it is," replied he.

They then lowered themselves from the window. I now rose lightly and cautiously, scarcely daring to breathe, from my place of concealment, and was creeping towards the door, when I heard my cousin's voice, in a sharp whisper, exclaim: "Scramble up again! G——d d——n you, you've forgot to lock the room-door!" and I perceived, by the straining of the rope which hung from above, that the mandate was instantly obeyed.

Not a second was to be lost. I passed through the door, which was only closed, and moved as rapidly as I could, consistently with stillness, along the lobby. Before I had gone many yards, I heard the door through which I had just passed double-locked on the inside. I glided down the stairs in terror, lest, at every corner, I should meet the murderer or one of his accomplices.

I reached the hall, and listened for a moment to ascertain whether all was silent around; no sound was audible. The parlor windows opened on the park, and through one of them I might, I thought, easily effect my escape. Accordingly, I hastily entered; but, to my consternation, a candle was burning in the room, and by its light I saw a figure seated at the dinner-table, upon which lay glasses, bottles, and the other accompaniments of a drinking-party. Two or three chairs were placed about the table irregularly, as if hastily abandoned by their occupants.

A single glance satisfied me that the figure was that of my French attendant. She was fast asleep, having probably drank deeply. There was something malignant and ghastly in the calmness of this bad woman's features, dimly illuminated as they were by the flickering blaze of the candle. A knife lay upon the table, and the terrible thought struck me — "Should I kill this sleeping accomplice in the guilt of the murderer, and thus secure my retreat?"

Nothing could be easier — it was but to draw the blade across her throat — the work of a second. An instant's pause, however, corrected me. "No," thought I, "the God who has conducted me thus far through the valley of the shadow of death, will not abandon me now. I will fall into their hands, or I will escape hence, but it shall be free from the stain of blood. His will be done."

I felt a confidence arising from this reflection, an assurance of protection which I cannot describe. There was no other means of escape, so I advanced, with a firm step and collected mind, to the window. I noiselessly withdrew the bars and unclosed the shutters — I pushed open the casement, and, without waiting to look behind me, I ran with my utmost speed, scarcely feeling the ground under me, down the avenue, taking care to keep upon the grass which bordered it.

I did not for a moment slack my speed, and I had now gained the center point between the park-gate and the mansion-house. Here the avenue made a wider circuit, and in order to avoid delay, I directed my way across the smooth sward round which the pathway wound, intending, at the opposite side of the flat, at a point which I distinguished by a group of old birch-trees, to enter again upon the beaten track, which was from thence tolerably direct to the gate.

I had, with my utmost speed, got about half way across this broad flat, when the rapid treading of a horse's hoofs struck upon my ear. My heart swelled in my bosom as though I would smother. The clattering of galloping hoofs approached — I was pursued — they were now upon the sward on which I was running —

there was not a bush or a bramble to shelter me — and, as if to render escape altogether desperate, the moon, which had hitherto been obscured, at this moment shone forth with a broad clear light, which made every object distinctly visible.

The sounds were now close behind me. I felt my knees bending under me, with the sensation which torments one in dreams. I reeled — I stumbled — I fell — and at the same instant the cause of my alarm wheeled past me at full gallop. It was one of the young fillies which pastured loose about the park, whose frolics had thus all but maddened me with terror. I scrambled to my feet, and rushed on with weak but rapid steps, my sportive companion still galloping round and round me with many a frisk and fling, until, at length, more dead than alive, I reached the avenue-gate and crossed the stile, I scarce knew how.

I ran through the village, in which all was silent as the grave, until my progress was arrested by the hoarse voice of a sentinel, who cried: "Who goes there?" I felt that I was now safe. I turned in the direction of the voice, and fell fainting at the soldier's feet. When I came to myself, I was sitting in a miserable hovel, surrounded by strange faces, all bespeaking curiosity and compassion.

Many soldiers were in it also: indeed, as I afterwards found, it was employed as a guard-room by a detachment of troops quartered for that night in the town. In a few words I informed their officer of the circumstances which had occurred, describing also the appearance of the persons engaged in the murder; and he, without loss of time, proceeded to the mansion-house of Carrickleigh, taking with him a party of his men. But the villains had discovered their mistake, and had effected their escape before the arrival of the military. The Frenchwoman was, however, arrested in the neighborhood upon the next day. She was tried and condemned upon the ensuing assizes; and previous to her execution, confessed that *"she had a hand in making Hugh Tisdal's bed."* She had been a housekeeper in the castle at the time, and a kind of *chère amie* of my uncle's. She was, in reality, able to speak English like a native, but had exclusively used the French language, I suppose to facilitate her disguise. She died the same hardened wretch which she had lived, confessing her crimes only, as she alleged, that her doing so might involve Sir Arthur T——n, the great author of her guilt and misery, and whom she now regarded with unmitigated detestation.

With the particulars of Sir Arthur's and his son's escape, as far as they are known, you are acquainted. You are also in possession of their after fate — the terrible, the tremendous retribution which, after long delays of many years, finally overtook and crushed them. Wonderful and inscrutable are the dealings of God with His creatures.

Deep and fervent as must always be my gratitude to heaven for my deliverance, effected by a chain of providential occurrences, the failing of a single link of which must have ensured my destruction, I was long before I could look back upon it with other feelings than those of bitterness, almost of agony.

The only being that had ever really loved me, my nearest and dearest friend, ever ready to sympathize, to counsel, and to assist — the gayest, the gentlest, the warmest heart — the only creature on earth that cared for me — *her* life had been the price of my deliverance; and I then uttered the wish, which no event of my long and sorrowful life has taught me to recall, that she had been spared, and that, in her stead, *I* were moldering in the grave, forgotten and at rest.

The Bridal of Carrigvarah

Being a Sixth Extract from the Legacy of the late Francis Purcell, P.P. of Drumcoolagh

*I*n a sequestered district of the county of Limerick, there stood my early life, some forty years ago, one of those strong stone buildings, half castle, half farmhouse, which are not infrequent in the South of Ireland, and whose solid masonry and massive construction seem to prove at once the insecurity and the caution of the Cromwellite settlers who erected them. At the time of which I speak, this building was tenanted by an elderly man, whose starch and puritanic mien and manners might have become the morose preaching parliamentarian captain who had raised the house and ruled the household more than a hundred years before; but this man, though Protestant by descent as by name, was not so in religion; he was a strict, and in outward observances, an exemplary Catholic; his father had returned in early youth to the true faith, and died in the bosom of the church.

Martin Heathcote was, at the time of which I speak, a widower, but his housekeeping was not on that account altogether solitary, for he had a daughter whose age was now sufficiently advanced to warrant her father in imposing upon her the grave duties of domestic superintendence.

This little establishment was perfectly isolated, and very little intruded upon by acts of neighborhood; for the rank of its occupants was of that equivocal kind which precludes all familiar association with those of a decidedly inferior rank, while it is not sufficient to entitle its possessors to the society of established gentility, among whom the nearest residents were the O'Maras of Carrigvarah, whose mansion-house, constructed out of the ruins of an old abbey whose towers and cloisters had been leveled by the shot of Cromwell's artillery, stood not half a mile lower upon the river banks.

Colonel O'Mara, the possessor of the estates, was then in a declining state of health, and absent with his lady from the country, leaving at the castle his son young O'Mara, and a kind of humble companion named Edward Dwyer, who, if report belied him not, had done in his early days some *peculiar services* for the Colonel, who had been a gay man — perhaps worse — but enough of recapitulation.

It was in the autumn of the year 17—— that the events which led to the catastrophe which I have to detail occurred. I shall run through the said recital as briefly as clearness will permit, and leave you to moralize, if such be your mood, upon the story of real life, which I even now trace at this distant period not without emotion.

It was upon a beautiful autumn evening, at that glad

period of the season when the harvest yields its abundance, that two figures were seen sauntering along the
banks of the winding river, which I described as bound-
ing the farm occupied by Heathcote; they had been, as
the rods and landing-nets which they listlessly carried
went to show, plying the gentle but in this case not
altogether solitary craft of the fisherman. One of those
persons was a tall and singularly handsome young
man, whose dark hair and complexion might almost
have belonged to a Spaniard, as might also the proud
but melancholy expression which gave to his countenance a character which contrasts sadly, but not unin-
terestingly, with extreme youth; his air, as he spoke with
his companion, was marked by that careless familiarity
which denotes a conscious superiority of one kind or
other, or which may be construed into a species of
contempt; his comrade afforded to him in every respect
a striking contrast. He was rather low in stature — a
defect which was enhanced by a broad and square-built
figure — his face was sallow, and his features had that
prominence and sharpness which frequently accompany personal deformity — a remarkably wide mouth,
with teeth white as the fangs of a wolf, and a pair of
quick, dark eyes, whose effect was heightened by the
shadow of a heavy black brow, gave to his face a power
of expression, particularly when sarcastic or malignant
emotions were to be exhibited, which features regularly
handsome could scarcely have possessed.

"Well, sir," said the latter personage, "I have lived in
hall and abbey, town and country, here and abroad for
forty years and more, and should know a thing or two,
and as I am a living man, I swear I think the girl loves
you."

"You are a fool, Ned," said the younger.

"I may be a fool," replied the first speaker, "in
matters where my own advantage is staked, but my eye

is keen enough to see through the flimsy disguise of a country damsel at a glance; and I tell you, as surely as I hold this rod, the girl loves you."

"Oh I this is downright headstrong folly," replied the young fisherman. "Why, Ned, you try to persuade me against my reason, that the event which is most to be deprecated has actually occurred. She is, no doubt, a pretty girl — a beautiful girl — but I have not lost my heart to her; and why should I wish her to be in love with me? Tush, man, the days of romance are gone, and a young gentleman may talk, and walk, and laugh with a pretty country maiden, and never breathe aspirations, or vows, or sighs about the matter; unequal matches are much oftener read of than made, and the man who could, even in thought, conceive a wish against the honor of an unsuspecting, artless girl, is a villain, for whom hanging is too good."

This concluding sentence was uttered with an animation and excitement, which the mere announcement of an abstract moral sentiment could hardly account for.

"You are, then, indifferent, honestly and in sober earnest, indifferent to the girl?" inquired Dwyer.

"Altogether so," was the reply.

"Then I have a request to make," continued Dwyer, "and I may as well urge it now as at any other time. I have been for nearly twenty years the faithful, and by no means useless, servant of your family; you know that I have rendered your father critical and important services —" he paused, and added hastily: "you are not in the mood — I tire you, sir."

"Nay," cried O'Mara, "I listen patiently — proceed."

"For all these services, and they were not, as I have said, few or valueless, I have received little more reward than liberal promises; you have told me often that this should be mended — I'll make it easily done — I'm not unreasonable — I should be contented to hold Heath-cote's ground, along with this small farm on which we stand, as full quittance of all obligations and promises between us."

"But how the devil can I effect that for you; this farm, it is true, I, or my father, rather, may lease to you, but Heathcote's title we cannot impugn; and even if we could, you would not expect us to ruin an honest man, in order to make way for *you*, Ned."

"What I am," replied Dwyer, with the calmness of one who is so accustomed to contemptuous insinuations as to receive them with perfect indifference, "is to be attributed to my devotedness to your honorable family — but that is neither here nor there. I do not ask you to displace Heathcote, in order to made room for me. I know it is out of your power to do so. Now hearken to me for a moment; Heathcote's property, that which he has set out to tenants, is worth, say in rents, at most, one hundred pounds: half of this yearly amount is assigned to your father, until payment be made of a bond for a thousand pounds, with interest and so forth. Hear me patiently for a moment and I have done. Now go you to Heathcote, and tell him your father will burn the bond, and cancel the debt, upon one condition — that when I am in possession of this farm, which you can lease to me on what terms you think suitable, he will convey over his property to me, reserving what life-interest may appear fair, I engaging at the same time to marry his daughter, and make such settlements upon her as shall be thought fitting — he is not a fool — the man will close with the offer."

O'Mara turned shortly upon Dwyer, and gazed upon him for a moment with an expression of almost unmixed resentment.

"How," said he at length, "*you* contract to marry

Ellen Heathcote? the poor, innocent, confiding, light-hearted girl. No, no, Edward Dwyer, I know you too well for that — your services, be they what they will, must not, shall not go unrewarded — your avarice shall be appeased — but not with a human sacrifice! Dwyer, I speak to you without disguise; you know me to be acquainted with your history, and what's more, with your character. Now tell me frankly, were I to do as you desire me, in cool blood, should I not prove myself a more uncompromising and unfeeling villain than humanity even in its most monstrous shapes has ever yet given birth to?"

Dwyer met this impetuous language with the unmoved and impenetrable calmness which always marked him when excitement would have appeared in others; he even smiled as he replied: (and Dwyer's smile, for I have seen it, was characteristically of that unfortunate kind which implies, as regards the emotions of others, not sympathy but derision).

"This eloquence goes to prove Ellen Heathcote something nearer to your heart than your great indifference would have led me to suppose."

There was something in the tone, perhaps in the truth of the insinuation, which at once kindled the quick pride and the anger of O'Mara, and he instantly replied:

"Be silent, sir, this is insolent folly."

Whether it was that Dwyer was more keenly interested in the success of his suit, or more deeply disappointed at its failure than he cared to express, or that he was in a less complacent mood than was his wont, it is certain that his countenance expressed more emotion at this direct insult than it had ever exhibited before under similar circumstances; for his eyes gleamed for an instant with savage and undisguised ferocity upon the young man, and a dark glow crossed his brow, and for the moment he looked about to spring at the throat of his insolent patron; but the impulse whatever it might be, was quickly suppressed, and before O'Mara had time to detect the scowl, it had vanished.

"Nay, sir," said Dwyer, "I meant no offence, and I will take none, at your hands at least. I will confess I care not, in love and so forth, a single bean for the girl; she was the mere channel through which her father's wealth, if such a pittance deserves the name, was to have flowed into my possession — 'twas in respect of your family finances the most economical provision for myself which I could devise — a matter in which you, not I, are interested. As for women, they are all pretty much alike to me. I am too old myself to make nice distinctions, and too ugly to succeed by Cupid's arts; and when a man despairs of success, he soon ceases to care for it. So, if you know me, as you profess to do, rest satisfied '*cæteris paribus*;' the money part of the transaction being equally advantageous, I should regret the loss of Ellen Heathcote just as little as I should the escape of a minnow from my landing-net."

They walked on for a few minutes in silence, which was not broken till Dwyer, who had climbed a stile in order to pass a low stone wall which lay in their way, exclaimed:

"By the rood, she's here — how like a philosopher you look."

The conscious blood mounted to O'Mara's cheek; he crossed the stile, and, separated from him only by a slight fence and a gate, stood the subject of their recent and somewhat angry discussion.

"God save you, Miss Heathcote," cried Dwyer, approaching the gate.

The salutation was cheerfully returned, and before anything more could pass, O'Mara had joined the party.

My friend, that you may understand the strength and depth of those impetuous passions, that you may account for the fatal infatuation which led to the catastrophe which I have to relate, I must tell you, that though I have seen the beauties of cities and of courts, with all the splendor of studied ornament about them to enhance their graces, possessing charms which had made them known almost throughout the world, and worshipped with the incense of a thousand votaries, yet never, nowhere did I behold a being of such exquisite and touching beauty, as that possessed by the creature of whom I have just spoken. At the moment of which I write, she was standing near the gate, close to which several brown-armed, rosy-cheeked damsels were engaged in milking the peaceful cows, who stood picturesquely grouped together. She had just thrown back the hood. which is the graceful characteristic of the Irish girl's attire, so that her small and classic head was quite uncovered, save only by the dark-brown hair, which with graceful simplicity was parted above her forehead. There was nothing to shade the clearness of her beautiful complexion; the delicately-formed features, so exquisite when taken singly, so indescribable when combined, so purely artless, yet so meet for all expression. She was a thing so very beautiful, you could not look on her without feeling your heart touched as by sweet music. Whose lightest action was a grace — whose lightest word a spell — no limner's art, though ne'er so perfect, could shadow forth her beauty; and do I dare with feeble words try to make you see it?* Providence is indeed no respecter of persons, its bless-

---

* Father Purcell seems to have had an admiration for the beauties of nature, particularly as developed in the fair sex; a habit of mind which has been rather improved upon than discontinued by his successors from Maynooth. — ED.

ings and its inflictions are apportioned with an undist-
inguishing hand, and until the race is over, and life be
done, none can know whether those perfections, which
seemed its goodliest gifts, many not prove its most
fatal; but enough of this.

Dwyer strolled carelessly onward by the banks of the
stream, leaving his young companion leaning over the
gate in close and interesting parlance with Ellen Heathcote; as he moved on, he half thought, half uttered
words to this effect:

"Insolent young spawn of ingratitude and guilt, how
long must I submit to be trod upon thus; and yet why
should I murmur — his day is even now declining —
and if I live a year, I shall see the darkness cover him
and his forever. Scarce half his broad estates shall save
him — but I must wait — I am but a pauper now — a
beggar's accusation is always a libel — they must reward
me soon — and were I independent once, I'd make
them feel my power, and feel it *so,* that I should die the
richest or the best avenged servant of a great man that
has ever been heard of — yes, I must wait — I must make
sure of something at least — I must be able to stand by
myself — and then — and then —" He clutched his
fingers together, as if in the act of strangling the object
of his hatred. "But one thing shall save him — but one
thing only — he shall pay me my own price — and if
he acts liberally, as no doubt he will do, upon compul-
sion, why he saves his reputation — perhaps his neck
— the insolent young whelp yonder would speak in an
humbler key if he but knew his father's jeopardy — but
all in good time."

He now stood upon the long, steep, narrow bridge,
which crossed the river close to Carrigvarah, the family
mansion of the O'Maras; he looked back in the direction in which he had left his companion, and leaning
upon the battlement, he ruminated long and moodily.

At length he raised himself and said:

"He loves the girl, and *will* love her more — I. have an opportunity of winning favor, of doing service, which shall bind him to me; yes, he shall have the girl, if I have art to compass the matter. I must think upon it."

He entered the avenue and was soon lost in the distance.

Days and weeks passed on, and young O'Mara daily took his rod and net, and rambled up the river; and scarce twelve hours elapsed in which some of those accidents, which invariably bring lovers together, did not secure him a meeting of longer or shorter duration, with the beautiful girl whom he so fatally loved.

One evening, after a long interview with her, in which he had been almost irresistibly prompted to declare his love, and had all but yielded himself up to the passionate impulse, upon his arrival at home he found a letter on the table awaiting his return; it was from his father to the following effect:

"*To Richard O'Mara.*
"September, 17——, L——m, England.
"My Dear Son, —

"I have just had a severe attack of my old and almost forgotten enemy, the gout. This I regard as a good sign; the doctors telling me that it is the safest development of peccant humors; and I think my chest is less tormenting and oppressed than I have known it for some years. My chief reason for writing to you now, as I do it not without difficulty, is to let you know my pleasure in certain matters, in which I suspect some shameful, and, indeed, infatuated neglect on your part, '*quem perdere vult deus prius dementat:*' how comes it that you have neglected to write to Lady Emily or any of that family? the understood relation subsisting between you is one of extreme delicacy, and which calls for marked and courteous, nay, devoted attention upon your side. Lord —— is already offended; beware what you do; for as you will find, if this match be lost by your fault or folly, by —— I will cut you off with a shilling. I am not in the habit of using threats when I do not mean to fulfill them, and that you well know; however I do not think you have much real cause for alarm in this case. Lady Emily, who, by the way, looks if possible more charming than ever, is anything but hard-hearted, at least when *you* solicit; but do as I desire, and lose no time in making what excuse you may, and let me hear from you when you can fix a time to join me and your mother here.

"Your sincere well-wisher and father,
"Richard O'Mara."

In this letter was enclosed a smaller one, directed to Dwyer, and containing a check for twelve pounds, with the following words:

"Make use of the enclosed, and let me hear if Richard is upon any wild scheme at present: I am uneasy about him, and not without reason; report to me speedily the result of your vigilance.

"R. O'Mara."

Dwyer just glanced through this brief, but not unwelcome, epistle; and deposited it and its contents in the secret recesses of his breeches pocket, and then fixed his eyes upon the face of his companion, who sat opposite, utterly absorbed in the perusal of his father's letter, which he read again and again, pausing and muttering between whiles, and apparently lost in no very pleasing reflections. At length he very abruptly exclaimed:

"A delicate epistle, truly — and a politic — would that my tongue had been burned through before I assented to that doubly-cursed contract. Why, I am not pledged yet — I am not; there is neither writing, nor troth, nor word of honor, passed between us. My father has no right to pledge me, even though I told him I liked the girl, and would wish the match. 'Tis not enough that my father offers her my heart and hand; he has no right to do it; a delicate woman would not accept professions made by proxy. Lady Emily! Lady Emily! with all the tawdry frippery, and finery of dress and demeanor — compare *her* with —— Pshaw! Ridiculous! How blind, how idiotic I have been."

He relapsed into moody reflections, which Dwyer did not care to disturb, and some ten minutes might have passed before he spoke again. When he did, it was in the calm tone of one who has irrevocably resolved upon some decided and important act.

"Dwyer," he said, rising and approaching that person, "whatever god or demon told you, even before my own heart knew it, that I loved Ellen Heathcote, spoke truth. I love her madly — I never dreamed till now how fervently, how irrevocably, I am hers — how dead to me all other interests are Dwyer, I know something of your disposition, and you no doubt think it strange that I should tell to you, of all persons, *such* a secret; but whatever be your faults, I think you are attached to our family. I am satisfied you will not betray me. I know —"

"Pardon me," said Dwyer, "if I say that great professions of confidence too frequently mark distrust. I have no possible motive to induce me to betray you; on the contrary, I would gladly assist and direct whatever plans you may have formed. Command me as you please; I have said enough."

"I will not doubt you, Dwyer," said O'Mara; " I have

taken my resolution — I have, I think, firmness to act up to it. To marry Ellen Heathcote, situated as I am, were madness; to propose anything else were worse, were villainy not to be named. I will leave the country tomorrow, cost what pain it may, for England. I will at once break off the proposed alliance with Lady Emily, and will wait until I am my own master, to open my heart to Ellen. My father may say and do what he likes; but his passion will not last. He will forgive me; and even were he to disinherit me, as he threatens, there is some property which must descend to me, which his will cannot affect. He cannot ruin my interests; he *shall not* ruin my happiness. Dwyer, give me pen and ink; I will write this moment."

This bold plan of proceeding for many reasons appeared inexpedient to Dwyer, and he determined not to consent to its adoption without a struggle.

"I commend your prudence," said he, "in determining to remove yourself from the fascinating influence which has so long bound you here; but beware of offending your father. Colonel O'Mara is not a man to forgive an act of deliberate disobedience, and surely you are not mad enough to ruin yourself with him by offering an outrageous insult to Lady Emily and to her family in her person; therefore you must not break off the understood contract which subsists between you by any formal act — hear me out patiently. You must let Lady Emily perceive, as you easily may, without rudeness or even coldness of manner, that she is perfectly indifferent to you; and when she understands this to be the case, it she possesses either delicacy or spirit, she will herself break off the engagement. Make what delay it is possible to effect; it is very possible that your father, who cannot, in all probability, live many months, may not live as many days if harassed and excited by such scenes as your breaking off your engagement must produce."

"Dwyer," said O'Mara, "I will hear you out — proceed."

"Besides, sir, remember," he continued, "the understanding which we have termed an engagement was entered into without any direct sanction upon your part; your father has committed *himself,* not *you,* to Lord ——. Before a real contract can subsist, you must be an assenting party to it. I know of no casuistry subtle enough to involve you in any engagement whatever, without such an ingredient. Tush! you have an easy card to play."

"Well," said the young man, "I will think on what you have said; in the meantime, I will write to my father to announce my immediate departure, in order to join him."

"Excuse me," said Dwyer, "but I would suggest that by hastening your departure you but bring your dangers nearer. While you are in this country a letter now and then keeps everything quiet; but once across the Channel and with the colonel, you must either quarrel with him to your own destruction, or you must dance attendance upon Lady Emily with such assiduity as to commit yourself as completely as if you had been thrice called with her in the parish church. No, no; keep to this side of the Channel as long as you decently can. Besides, your sudden departure must appear suspicious, and will probably excite inquiry. Every good end likely to be accomplished by your absence will be effected as well by your departure for Dublin, where you may remain for three weeks or a month without giving rise to curiosity or doubt of an unpleasant kind; I would therefore advise you strongly to write immediately to the colonel, stating that business has occurred to defer your departure for a month, and you can then leave this place, if you think fit, immediately, that is, within a week or so."

Young O'Mara was not hard to be persuaded. Perhaps it was that, unacknowledged by himself, any argument which recommended his staying, even for an hour longer than his first decision had announced, in the neighborhood of Ellen Heathcote, appeared peculiarly cogent and convincing; however this may have been, it is certain that he followed the counsel of his cool-headed follower, who retired that night to bed with the pleasing conviction that he was likely soon to involve his young patron in all the intricacies of disguise and intrigue — a consummation which would leave him totally at the mercy of the favored confidant who should possess his secret.

Young O'Mara's reflections were more agitating and less satisfactory than those of his companion. He resolved upon leaving the country before two days had passed. He felt that he could not fairly seek to involve Ellen Heathcote in his fate by pledge or promise, until he had extricated himself from those trammels which constrained and embarrassed all his actions. His determination was so far prudent; but, alas! he also resolved that it was but right, but necessary, that he should see her before his departure. His leaving the country without a look or a word of parting kindness interchanged, must to her appear an act of cold and heartless caprice; he could not bear the thought.

"No," said he, "I am not child enough to say more than prudence tells me I ought to say; this cowardly distrust of my firmness I should and will contemn. Besides, why should I commit myself? It is possible the girl may not care for me. No, no; I need not shrink from this interview. I have no reason to doubt my firmness — none — none. I must cease to be governed by impulse. I am involved in rocks and quicksands; and a collected spirit, a quick eye, and a steady hand, alone can pilot me through. God grant me a safe voyage!"

The next day came, and young O'Mara did not take his fishing-rod as usual, but wrote two letters; the one to his father, announcing his intention of departing speedily for England; the other to Lady Emily, containing a cold but courteous apology for his apparent neglect. Both these were dispatched to the post office that evening, and upon the next morning he was to leave the country.

Upon the night of the momentous day of which we have just spoken, Ellen Heathcote glided silently and unperceived from among the busy crowds who were engaged in the gay dissipation furnished by what is in Ireland commonly called a dance (the expenses attendant upon which, music, etc., are defrayed by a subscription of one halfpenny each), and having drawn her mantle closely about her, was proceeding with quick steps to traverse the small field which separated her from her father's abode. She had not walked many yards when she became aware that a solitary figure, muffled in a cloak, stood in the pathway. It approached; a low voice whispered:

"Ellen."

"Is it you, Master Richard?" she replied.

He threw back the cloak which had concealed his features.

"It is I, Ellen, he said; "I have been watching for you. I will not delay you long."

He took her hand, and she did not attempt to withdraw it; for she was too artless to think any evil, too confiding to dread it.

"Ellen," he continued, even now unconsciously departing from the rigid course which prudence had marked out; "Ellen, I am going to leave the country; going tomorrow. I have had letters from England. I must go; and the sea will soon be between us."

He paused, and she was silent.

"There is one request, one entreaty I have to make," he continued; "I would, when I am far away, have something to look at which belonged to you. Will you give me — do not refuse it — one little lock of your beautiful hair?"

With artless alacrity, but with trembling hand, she took the scissors, which in simple fashion hung by her side, and detached one of the long and beautiful locks which parted over her forehead. She placed it in his hand.

Again he took her hand, and twice he attempted to speak in vain; at length he said:

"Ellen, when I am gone — when I am away — will you sometimes remember, sometimes think of me?"

Ellen Heathcote had as much, perhaps more, of what is noble in pride than the haughtiest beauty that ever trod a court; but the effort was useless; the honest struggle was in vain; and she burst into floods of tears, bitterer than she had ever shed before.

I cannot tell how passions rise and fall; I cannot describe the impetuous words of the young lover, as pressing again and again to his lips the cold, passive hand, which had been resigned to him, prudence, caution, doubts, resolutions, all vanished from his view, and melted into nothing. 'Tis for me to tell the simple fact, that from that brief interview they both departed promised and pledged to each other forever.

Through the rest of this story events follow one another rapidly.

A few nights after that which I have just mentioned, Ellen Heathcote disappeared; but her father was not left long in suspense as to her fate, for Dwyer, accompanied by one of those mendicant friars who traversed the country then even more commonly than they now do, called upon Heathcote before he had had time to take any active measures for the recovery of his child, and put him in possession of a document which appeared to contain satisfactory evidence of the marriage of Ellen Heathcote with Richard O'Mara, executed upon the evening previous, as the date went to show; and signed by both parties, as well as by Dwyer and a servant of young O'Mara's, both these having acted as witnesses; and further supported by the signature of Peter Nicholls, a brother of the order of St. Francis, by whom the ceremony had been performed, and whom Heathcote had no difficulty in recognizing in the person of his visitant.

This document, and the prompt personal visit of the two men, and above all, the known identity of the Franciscan, satisfied Heathcote as fully as anything short of complete publicity could have done. And his conviction was not a mistaken one.

Dwyer, before he took his leave, impressed upon Heathcote the necessity of keeping the affair so secret as to render it impossible that it should reach Colonel O'Mara's ears, an event which would have been attended with ruinous consequences to all parties. He refused, also, to permit Heathcote to see his daughter, and even to tell him where she was, until circumstances rendered it safe for him to visit her.

Heathcote was a harsh and sullen man; and though his temper was anything but tractable, there was so much to please, almost to dazzle him, in the event, that he accepted the terms which Dwyer imposed upon him without any further token of disapprobation than a shake of the head, and a gruff wish that "it might prove all for the best."

Nearly two months had passed, and young O'Mara had not yet departed for England. His letters had been strangely few and far between; and in short, his conduct was such as to induce Colonel O'Mara to hasten his return to Ireland, and at the same time to press an engagement, which Lord ——, his son Captain N——, and Lady Emily had made to spend some weeks with him at his residence in Dublin.

A letter arrived for young O'Mara, stating the arrangement, and requiring his attendance in Dublin, which was accordingly immediately afforded.

He arrived, with Dwyer, in time to welcome his father and his distinguished guests. He resolved to break off his embarrassing connection with Lady Emily, without, however, stating the real motive, which he felt would exasperate the resentment which his father and Lord —— would no doubt feel at his conduct.

He strongly felt how dishonorably he would act if, in obedience to Dwyer's advice, he seemed tacitly to acquiesce in an engagement which it was impossible for him to fulfill. He knew that Lady Emily was not capable of anything like strong attachment; and that even if she were, he had no reason whatever to suppose that she cared at all for him.

He had not at any time desired the alliance; nor had he any reason to suppose the young lady in any degree less indifferent. He regarded it now, and not without some appearance of justice, as nothing more than a kind of understood stipulation, entered into by their parents, and to be considered rather as a matter of business and calculation than as involving anything of mutual inclination on the part of the parties most nearly interested in the matter.

He anxiously, therefore, watched for an opportunity of making known his feelings to Lord ——, as he could not with propriety do so to Lady Emily; but what at a distance appeared to be a matter of easy accomplishment, now, upon a nearer approach, and when the immediate impulse which had prompted the act had subsided, appeared so full of difficulty and almost inextricable embarrassments, that he involuntarily shrunk from the task day after day.

Though it was a source of indescribable anxiety to him, he did not venture to write to Ellen, for he could not disguise from himself the danger which the secrecy of his connection with her must incur by his communicating with her, even through a public office, where their letters might be permitted to lie longer than the gossiping inquisitiveness of a country town would warrant him in supposing safe.

It was about a fortnight after young O'Mara had arrived in Dublin, where all things, and places, and amusements; and persons seemed thoroughly stale, flat, and unprofitable, when one day, tempted by the unusual fineness of the weather, Lady Emily proposed a walk in the College Park, a favorite promenade at that time. She therefore with young O'Mara, accompanied by Dwyer (who, by-the-by, when he pleased, could act the gentleman sufficiently well), proceeded to the place proposed, where they continued to walk for some time.

"Why, Richard," said Lady Emily, after a tedious and unbroken pause of some minutes, "you are becoming worse and worse every day. You are growing absolutely intolerable; perfectly stupid! not one good thing have I heard since I left the house."

O'Mara smiled, and was seeking for a suitable reply, when his design was interrupted, and his attention suddenly and painfully arrested, by the appearance of two figures, who were slowly passing the broad walk on which he and his party moved; the one was that of Captain N——, the other was the form of — Martin Heathcote!

O'Mara felt confounded, almost stunned; the anticipation of some impending mischief — of an immediate and violent collision with a young man whom he had ever regarded as his friend, were apprehensions which such a juxtaposition could not fail to produce.

"Is Heathcote mad?" thought he. "What devil can have brought him here?"

Dwyer having exchanged a significant glance with O'Mara, said slightly to Lady Emily:

"Will your ladyship excuse me for a moment? I have a word to say to Captain N——, and will, with your permission, immediately rejoin you."

He bowed, and walking rapidly on, was in a few moments beside the object of his and his patron's uneasiness.

Whatever Heathcote's object might be, he certainly had not yet declared the secret, whose safety O'Mara had so naturally desired, for Captain N—— appeared in good spirits; and on coming up to his sister and her companion, he joined them for a moment, telling O'Mara, laughingly, that an old quiz had come from the country for the express purpose of telling tales, as it was to be supposed, of him (young O'Mara), in whose neighborhood he lived.

During this speech it required all the effort which it was possible to exert to prevent O'Mara's betraying the extreme agitation to which his situation gave rise. Captain N——, however, suspected nothing, and passed on without further delay.

Dinner was an early meal in those days, and Lady Emily was obliged to leave the Park in less than half an hour after the unpleasant meeting which we have just mentioned.

Young O'Mara and, at a sign from him, Dwyer having escorted the lady to the door of Colonel O'Mara's house, pretended an engagement, and departed together.

Richard O'Mara instantly questioned his comrade

upon the subject of his anxiety; but Dwyer had nothing to communicate of a satisfactory nature. He had only time, while the captain had been engaged with Lady Emily and her companion, to say to Heathcote:

"Be secret, as you value your existence: everything will be right, if you be but secret."

To this Heathcote had replied: "Never fear me; I understand what I am about."

This was said in such an ambiguous manner that it was impossible to conjecture whether he intended or not to act upon Dwyer's exhortation. The conclusion which appeared most natural, was by no means an agreeable one.

It was much to be feared that Heathcote having heard some vague report of O'Mara's engagement with Lady Emily, perhaps exaggerated, by the repetition, into a speedily approaching marriage, had become alarmed for his daughter's interest, and had taken this decisive step in order to prevent, by a disclosure of the circumstances of his clandestine union with Ellen, the possibility of his completing a guilty alliance with Captain N——'s sister. If he entertained the suspicions which they attributed to him, he had certainly taken the most effectual means to prevent their being realized. Whatever his object might be, his presence in Dublin, in company with Captain N——, boded nothing good to O'Mara.

They entered ——'s tavern, in Dame Street, together; and there, over a hasty and by no means a comfortable meal, they talked over their plans and conjectures. Evening closed in, and found them still closeted together, with nothing to interrupt, and a large tankard of claret to sustain their desultory conversation.

Nothing had been determined upon, except that Dwyer and O'Mara should proceed under cover of the darkness to search the town for Heathcote, and by minute inquiries at the most frequented houses of entertainment, to ascertain his place of residence, in order to procuring a full and explanatory interview with him. They had each filled their last glass, and were sipping it slowly, seated with their feet stretched towards a bright cheerful fire; the small table which sustained the flagon of which we have spoken, together with two pair of wax candles, placed between them, so as to afford a convenient resting-place for the long glasses out of which they drank.

"One good result, at all events, will be effected by Heathcote's visit," said O'Mara. "Before twenty-four hours I shall do that which I should have done long ago. I shall, without reserve, state everything. I can no longer endure this suspense — this dishonorable secrecy — this apparent dissimulation. Every moment I have passed since my departure from the country has been one of embarrassment, of pain, of humiliation. Tomorrow I will brave the storm, whether successfully or not is doubtful; but I had rather walk the high roads a beggar, than submit a day longer to be made the degraded sport of every accident — the miserable dependent upon a successful system of deception. Though *passive* deception, it is still unmanly, unworthy, unjustifiable deception. I cannot bear to think of it. I despise myself, but I will cease to be the despicable thing I have become. Tomorrow sees me free, and this harassing subject forever at rest."

He was interrupted here by the sound of footsteps heavily but rapidly ascending the tavern staircase. The room door opened, and Captain N——, accompanied by a fashionably-attired young man, entered the room.

Young O'Mara had risen from his seat on the entrance of their unexpected visitants; and the moment Captain N—— recognized his person, an evident and ominous change passed over his countenance. He turned hastily to withdraw, but, as it seemed, almost instantly changed his mind, for he turned again abruptly.

"This chamber is engaged, sir," said the waiter.

"Leave the room, sir," was his only reply.

"The room is engaged, sir," repeated the waiter, probably believing that his first suggestion had been unheard.

"Leave the room, or go to hell!" shouted Captain N——; at the same time seizing the astounded waiter by the shoulder, he hurled him headlong into the passage, and flung the door to with a crash that shook the walls. "Sir," continued he, addressing himself to O'Mara, "I did not hope to have met you until tomorrow. Fortune has been kind to me — draw, and defend yourself."

At the same time he drew his sword, and placed himself in an attitude of attack.

"I will not draw upon *you*," said O'Mara. "I have, indeed, wronged you. I have given you just cause for resentment; but against your life I will never lift my hand."

"You are a coward, sir," replied Captain N——, with almost frightful vehemence, "as every trickster and swindler *is*. You are a contemptible dastard — a despicable, damned villain! Draw your sword, sir, and defend your life, or every post and pillar in this town shall tell your infamy."

"Perhaps," said his friend, with a sneer, "the gentleman can do better without his honor than without his wife."

"Yes," shouted the captain, "his wife — a trull — a common —"

"Silence, sir!" cried O'Mara, all the fierceness of his nature roused by this last insult — "your object is gained; your blood be upon your own head." At the same time he sprang across a bench which stood in his way, and pushing aside the table which supported the lights, in an instant their swords crossed, and they were engaged in close and deadly strife.

Captain N—— was far the stronger of the two; but, on the other hand, O'Mara possessed far more skill in the use of the fatal weapon which they employed. But the narrowness of the room rendered this advantage hardly available.

Almost instantly O'Mara received a slight wound upon the forehead, which, though little more than a scratch, bled so fast as to obstruct his sight considerably.

Those who have used the foil can tell how slight a derangement of eye or of hand is sufficient to determine a contest of this kind; and this knowledge will prevent their being surprised when I say, that, spite of O'Mara's superior skill and practice, his adversary's sword passed twice through and through his body, and he fell heavily and helplessly upon the floor of the chamber.

Without saying a word, the successful combatant quitted the room along with his companion, leaving Dwyer to shift as best he might for his fallen comrade.

With the assistance of some of the wondering menials of the place, Dwyer succeeded in conveying the wounded man into an adjoining room, where he was laid upon a bed, in a state bordering upon insensibility — the blood flowing, I might say *welling*, from the wounds so fast as to show that unless the bleeding were speedily and effectually stopped, he could not live for half an hour.

Medical aid was, of course, instantly procured, and Colonel O'Mara, though at the time seriously indisposed, was urgently requested to attend without loss of time. He did so; but human succor and support were all too late. The wound had been truly dealt — the tide of life had ebbed; and his father had not arrived five minutes when young O'Mara was a corpse. His body rests in the vaults of Christ Church, in Dublin, without a stone to mark the spot.

The counsels of the wicked are always dark, and their motives often beyond fathoming; and strange, unaccountable, incredible as it may seem, I do believe, and that upon evidence so clear as to amount almost to demonstration, that Heathcote's visit to Dublin — his betrayal of the secret — and the final and terrible catastrophe which laid O'Mara in the grave, were brought about by no other agent than Dwyer himself.

I have myself seen the letter which induced that visit. The handwriting is exactly what I have seen in other alleged specimens of Dwyer's penmanship. It is written with an affectation of honest alarm at O'Mara's conduct, and expresses a conviction that if some of Lady Emily's family be not informed of O'Mara's real situation, nothing could prevent his concluding with her an advantageous alliance, then upon the *tapis,* and altogether throwing off his allegiance to Ellen — a step which, as the writer candidly asserted, would finally conduce as inevitably to his own disgrace as it immediately would to her ruin and misery.

The production was formally signed with Dwyer's name, and the postscript contained a strict injunction of secrecy, asserting that if it were ascertained that such an epistle had been dispatched from such a quarter, it would be attended with the total ruin of the writer.

It is true that Dwyer, many years after, when this letter came to light, alleged it to be a forgery, an assertion whose truth, even to his dying hour, and long after he had apparently ceased to feel the lash of public scorn, he continued obstinately to maintain. Indeed this matter is full of mystery, for, revenge alone excepted, which I believe, in such minds as Dwyer's, seldom overcomes the sense of interest, the only intelligible motive which could have prompted him to such an act was the hope that since he had, through young O'Mara's interest, procured from the colonel a lease of a small farm upon the terms which he had originally stipulated, he might prosecute his plan touching the property of Martin Heathcote, rendering his daughter's hand free by the removal of young O'Mara. This appears to me too complicated a plan of villainy to have entered the mind even of such a man as Dwyer. I must, therefore, suppose his motives to have originated out of circumstances connected with this story which may not have come to my ear, and perhaps never will.

Colonel O'Mara felt the death of his son more deeply than I should have thought possible; but that son had been the last being who had continued to interest his cold heart. Perhaps the pride which he felt in his child had in it more of selfishness than of any generous feeling. But, be this as it may, the melancholy circumstances connected with Ellen Heathcote had reached him, and his conduct towards her proved, more strongly than anything else could have done, that he felt keenly and justly, and, to a certain degree, with a softened heart, the fatal event of which she had been, in some manner, alike the cause and the victim.

He evinced not towards her, as might have been expected, any unreasonable resentment. On the contrary, he exhibited great consideration, even tenderness, for her situation; and having ascertained where his son had placed her, he issued strict orders that she should not be disturbed, and that the fatal tidings, which had not yet reached her, should be withheld until they might be communicated in such a way as to soften as much as possible the inevitable shock.

These last directions were acted upon too scrupulously and too long; and, indeed, I am satisfied that had the event been communicated at once, however terrible and overwhelming the shock might have been, much of the bitterest anguish, of sickening doubts, of harassing suspense, would have been spared her, and the first tempestuous burst of sorrow having passed over, her chastened spirit might have recovered its tone, and her life have been spared. But the mistaken kindness which concealed from her the dreadful truth, instead of relieving her mind of a burden which it could not support, laid upon it a weight of horrible fears and doubts as to the affection of O'Mara, compared with which even the certainty of his death would have been tolerable.

One evening I had just seated myself beside a cheerful turf fire, with that true relish which a long cold ride through a bleak and shelterless country affords, stretching my chilled limbs to meet the genial influence, and imbibing the warmth at every pore, when my comfortable meditations were interrupted by a long and sonorous ringing at the doorbell evidently effected by no timid hand.

A messenger had arrived to request my attendance at the Lodge — such was the name which distinguished a small and somewhat antiquated building, occupying a peculiarly secluded position among the bleak and heathy hills which varied the surface of that not altogether uninteresting district, and which had, I believe, been employed by the keen and hardy ancestors of the O'Mara family as a convenient temporary residence during the sporting season.

Thither my attendance was required, in order to administer to a deeply distressed lady such comforts as an afflicted mind can gather from the sublime hopes and consolations of Christianity.

I had long suspected that the occupant of this se-

questered, I might say desolate, dwelling-house was the
poor girl whose brief story we are following; and feeling a keen interest in her fate — as who that had ever
seen her *did not?* — I started from my comfortable seat
with more eager alacrity than, I will confess it, I might
have evinced had my duty called me in another direction.

In a few minutes I was trotting rapidly onward,
preceded by my guide, who urged his horse with the
remorseless rapidity of one who seeks by the speed of
his progress to escape observation. Over roads and
through bogs we splashed and clattered, until at length
traversing the brow of a wild and rocky hill, whose
aspect seemed so barren and forbidding that it might
have been a lasting barrier alike to mortal sight and
step, the lonely building became visible, lying in a kind
of swampy flat, with a broad reedy pond or lake stretching away to its side, and backed by a farther range of
monotonous sweeping hills, marked with irregular
lines of grey rock, which, in the distance, bore a rude
and colossal resemblance to the walls of a fortification.

Riding with undiminished speed along a kind of
wild horse-track, we turned the corner of a high and
somewhat ruinous wall of loose stones, and making a
sudden wheel we found ourselves in a small quadrangle, surmounted on two sides by dilapidated stables
and kennels, on another by a broken stone wall, and
upon the fourth by the front of the lodge itself. The
whole character of the place was that of dreary deser-
tion and decay, which would of itself have predisposed
the mind for melancholy impressions. My guide dis-
mounted, and with respectful attention held my
horse's bridle while I got down; and knocking at the
door with the handle of his whip, it was speedily
opened by a neatly-dressed female domestic, and I was
admitted to the interior of the house, and conducted

into a small room, where a fire in some degree dispelled the cheerless air, which would otherwise have prevailed to a painful degree throughout the place.

I had been waiting but for a very few minutes when another female servant, somewhat older than the first, entered the room. She made some apology on the part of the person whom I had come to visit, for the slight delay which had already occurred, and requested me further to wait for a few minutes longer, intimating that the lady's grief was so violent, that without great effort she could not bring herself to speak calmly at all. As if to beguile the time, the good dame went on in a highly communicative strain to tell me, amongst much that could not interest me, a little of what I had desired to hear. I discovered that the grief of her whom I had come to visit was excited by the sudden death of a little boy, her only child, who was then lying dead in his mother's chamber.

"And the mother's name?" said I, inquiringly.

The woman looked at me for a moment, smiled, and shook her head with the air of mingled mystery and importance which seems to say, "I am unfathomable." I did not care to press the question, though I suspected that much of her apparent reluctance was affected, knowing that my doubts respecting the identity of the person whom I had come to visit must soon be set at rest, and after a little pause the worthy Abigail went on as fluently as ever. She told me that her young mistress had been, for the time she had been with her — that was, for about a year and a half — in declining health and spirits, and that she had loved her little child to a degree beyond expression — so devotedly that she could not, in all probability, survive it long.

While she was running on in this way the bell rang, and signing me to follow, she opened the room door, but stopped in the hall, and taking me a little aside, and speaking in a whisper, she told me, as I valued the life of the poor lady, not to say one word of the death of young O'Mara. I nodded acquiescence, and ascending a narrow and ill-constructed staircase, she stopped at a chamber door and knocked.

"Come in," said a gentle voice from within, and, preceded by my conductress, I entered a moderately-sized, but rather gloomy chamber.

There was but one living form within it — it was the light and graceful figure of a young woman. She had risen as I entered the room; but owing to the obscurity of the apartment, and to the circumstance that her face, as she looked towards the door, was turned away from the light, which found its way in dimly through the narrow windows, I could not instantly recognize the features.

"You do not remember me, sir?" said the same low, mournful voice. "I am — I *was* — Ellen Heathcote."

"I do remember you, my poor child," said I, taking her hand; "I do remember you very well. Speak to me frankly — speak to me as a friend. Whatever I can do or say for you, is yours already; only speak."

"You were always very kind, sir, to those — to those that *wanted* kindness."

The tears were almost overflowing, but she checked them; and as if an accession of fortitude had followed the momentary weakness, she continued, in a subdued but firm tone, to tell me briefly the circumstances of her marriage with O'Mara. When she had concluded the recital, she paused for a moment; and I asked again:

"Can I aid you in any way — by advice or otherwise?"

"I wish, sir, to tell you all I have been thinking about," she continued. "I am sure, sir, that Master Richard loved me once — I am sure he did not think to deceive me; but there were bad, hard-hearted people about him, and his family were all rich and high, and

I am sure he wishes *now* that he had never, never seen me. Well, sir, it is not in my heart to blame him. What was *I* that I should look at him? — an ignorant, poor, country girl — and he so high and great, and so beautiful. The blame was all mine — it was all my fault; I could not think or hope he would care for me more than a little time. Well, sir, I thought over and over again that since his love was gone from me forever, I should not stand in his way, and hinder whatever great thing his family wished for him. So I thought often and often to write him a letter to get the marriage broken, and to send me home; but for one reason, I would have done it long ago: there was a little child, his and mine — the dearest, the loveliest." She could not go on for a minute or two. "The little child that is lying there, on that bed; but it is dead and gone, and there is no reason *now* why I should delay any more about it."

She put her hand into her breast, and took out a letter, which she opened. She put it into my hands. It ran thus:

"Dear Master Richard,

"My little child is dead, and your happiness is all I care about now. Your marriage with me is displeasing to your family, and I would be a burden to you, and in your way in the fine places, and among the great friends where you must be. You ought, therefore, to break the marriage, and I will sign whatever *you* wish, or your family. I will never try to blame you, Master Richard — do not think it — for I never deserved your love, and must not complain now that I have lost it; but I will always pray for you, and be thinking of you while I live."

While I read this letter, I was satisfied that so far from adding to the poor girl's grief, a full disclosure of what had happened would, on the contrary, mitigate her sorrow, and deprive it of its sharpest sting.

"Ellen," said I solemnly, "Richard O'Mara was never unfaithful to you; he is now where human reproach can reach him no more."

As I said this, the hectic flush upon her cheek gave place to a paleness so deadly, that I almost thought she would drop lifeless upon the spot.

"Is he — is he dead, then?" said she, wildly.

I took her hand in mine, and told her the sad story as best I could. She listened with a calmness which appeared almost unnatural, until I had finished the mournful narration. She then arose, and going to the bedside, she drew the curtain and gazed silently and fixedly on the quiet face of the child: but the feelings which swelled at her heart could not be suppressed; the tears gushed forth, and sobbing as if her heart would break, she leant over the bed and took the dead child in her arms. She wept and kissed it, and kissed it and wept again, in grief so passionate, so heartrending, as to draw bitter tears from my eyes. I said what little I could to calm her — to have sought to do more would have been a mockery; and observing that the darkness had closed in, I took my leave and departed, being favored with the services of my former guide.

I expected to have been soon called upon again to visit the poor girl; but the Lodge lay beyond the boundary of my parish, and I felt a reluctance to trespass upon the precincts of my brother minister, and a certain degree of hesitation in intruding upon one whose situation was so very peculiar, and who would, I had no doubt, feel no scruple in requesting my attendance if she desired it.

A month, however, passed away, and I did not hear anything of Ellen. I called at the Lodge, and to my inquiries they answered that she was very much worse in health, and that since the death of the child she had been sinking fast, and so weak that she had been chiefly confined to her bed. I sent frequently to inquire, and often called myself, and all that I heard convinced me that she was rapidly sinking into the grave.

Late one night I was summoned from my rest, by a visit from the person who had upon the former occasion acted as my guide; he had come to summon me to the deathbed of her whom I had then attended. With all celerity I made my preparations, and, not without considerable difficulty and some danger, we made a rapid night-ride to the Lodge, a distance of five miles at least. We arrived safely, and in a very short time — but too late.

I stood by the bed upon which lay the once beautiful form of Ellen Heathcote. The brief but sorrowful trial was past — the desolate mourner was gone to that land where the pangs of grief, the tumults of passion, regrets and cold neglect, are felt no more. I leant over the lifeless face, and scanned the beautiful features which, living, had wrought such magic on all that looked upon them. They were, indeed, much wasted; but it was impossible for the fingers of death or of decay altogether to obliterate the traces of that exquisite beauty which had so distinguished her. As I gazed on this most sad and striking spectacle, remembrances thronged fast upon my mind, and tear after tear fell upon the cold form that slept tranquilly and forever. A few days afterwards I was told that a funeral had left the Lodge at the dead of night, and had been conducted with the most scrupulous secrecy. It was, of course, to me no mystery.

Heathcote lived to a very advanced age, being of that hard mould which is not easily impressionable. The selfish and the hard-hearted survive where nobler, more generous, and, above all, more sympathizing natures would have sunk forever.

Dwyer certainly succeeded in extorting, I cannot say how, considerable and advantageous leases from Colonel O'Mara; but after his death he disposed of his interest in these, and having for a time launched into a sea of profligate extravagance, he became bankrupt, and for a long time I totally lost sight of him.

The rebellion of '98, and the events which immediately followed, called him forth from his lurking-places, in the character of an informer; and I myself have seen the hoary-headed, paralytic perjurer, with a scowl of derision and defiance, brave the hootings and the execrations of the indignant multitude.

Strange
Events in the Life
of Schalken the Painter

Being a Seventh Extract from the Legacy of the late Francis Purcell, P.P. of Drumcoolagh

You will no doubt be surprised, my dear friend, at the subject of the following narrative. What had I to do with Schalken, or Schalken with me? He had returned to his native land, and was probably dead and buried, before I was born; I never visited Holland nor spoke with a native of that country. So much I believe you already know. I must, then, give you my authority, and state to you frankly the ground upon which rests the credibility of the strange story which I am, about to lay before you.

I was acquainted, in my early days, with a Captain Vandael, whose father had served King William in the Low Countries, and also in my own unhappy land during the Irish campaigns. I know not how it happened that I liked this man's society, spite of his politics and religion: but so it was; and it was by means of the free intercourse to which our intimacy gave rise that I became possessed of the curious tale which you are about to hear.

I had often been struck, while visiting Vandael, by a remarkable picture, in which, though no *connoisseur* myself, I could not fail to discern some very strong peculiarities, particularly in the distribution of light and shade, as also a certain oddity in the design itself, which interested my curiosity. It represented the interior of what might be a chamber in some antique religious building — the foreground was occupied by a female figure, arrayed in a species of white robe, part of which is arranged so as to form a veil. The dress, however, is not strictly that of any religious order. In its hand the figure bears a lamp, by whose light alone the form and face are illuminated; the features are marked by an arch smile, such as pretty women wear when engaged in successfully practicing some roguish trick; in the background, and, excepting where the dim red light of an expiring fire serves to define the form, totally in the shade, stands the figure of a man equipped in the old fashion, with doublet and so forth, in an attitude of alarm, his hand being placed upon the hilt of his sword, which he appears to be in the act of drawing.

"There are some pictures," said I to my friend, "which impress one, I know not how, with a conviction that they represent not the mere ideal shapes and combinations which have floated through the imagination of the artist, but scenes, faces, and situations which have actually existed. When I look upon that picture, something assures me that I behold the representation of a reality."

Vandael smiled, and, fixing his eyes upon the painting musingly, he said:

"Your fancy has not deceived you, my good friend, for that picture is the record, and I believe a faithful one, of a remarkable and mysterious occurrence. It was painted by Schalken, and contains, in the face of the female figure, which occupies the most prominent place in the design, an accurate portrait of Rose Velderkaust, the niece of Gerard Douw, the first and, I believe, the only love of Godfrey Schalken. My father knew the painter well, and from Schalken himself he learned the story of the mysterious drama, one scene of which the picture has embodied. This painting, which is accounted a fine specimen of Schalken's style, was bequeathed to my father by the artist's will, and, as you have observed, is a very striking and interesting production."

I had only to request Vandael to tell the story of the painting in order to be gratified; and thus it is that I am enabled to submit to you a faithful recital of what I heard myself, leaving you to reject or to allow the evidence upon which the truth of the tradition depends, with this one assurance, that Schalken was an honest, blunt Dutchman, and, I believe, wholly incapable of committing a flight of imagination; and further, that Vandael, from whom I heard the story, appeared firmly convinced of its truth.

There are few forms upon which the mantle of mystery and romance could seem to hang more ungracefully than upon that of the uncouth and clownish Schalken — the Dutch boor — the rude and dogged, but most cunning worker in oils, whose pieces delight the initiated of the present day almost as much as his manners disgusted the refined of his own; and yet this man, so rude, so dogged, so slovenly, I had almost said so savage, in mien and manner, during his after successes, had been selected by the capricious goddess, in his early life, to figure as the hero of a romance by no means devoid of interest or of mystery.

Who can tell how meet he may have been in his young days to play the part of the lover or of the hero — who can say that in early life he had been the same harsh, unlicked, and rugged boor that, in his maturer age, he proved — or how far the neglected rudeness which afterwards marked his air, and garb, and manners, may not have been the growth of that reckless apathy not infrequently produced by bitter misfortunes and disappointments in early life?

These questions can never now be answered.

We must content ourselves, then, with a plain statement of facts, or what have been received and transmitted as such, leaving matters of speculation to those who like them.

When Schalken studied under the immortal Gerard Douw, he was a young man; and in spite of the phlegmatic constitution and unexcitable manner which he shared, we believe, with his countrymen, he was not incapable of deep and vivid impressions, for it is an established fact that the young painter looked with considerable interest upon the beautiful niece of his wealthy master.

Rose Velderkaust was very young, having, at the period of which we speak, not yet attained her seventeenth year, and, if tradition speaks truth, possessed all the soft dimpling charms of the fail; light-haired Flemish maidens. Schalken had not studied long in the school of Gerard Douw, when he felt this interest deepening into something of a keener and intenser feeling than was quite consistent with the tranquility of his honest Dutch heart; and at the same time he perceived, or thought he perceived, flattering symptoms of a reciprocity of liking, and this was quite sufficient to determine whatever indecision he might have heretofore experienced, and to lead him to devote exclusively to her every hope and feeling of his heart. In short, he was as much in love as a Dutchman could be. He was not long in making his passion known to the pretty maiden herself, and his declaration was followed by a corresponding confession upon her part.

Schalken, however, was a poor man, and he possessed no counterbalancing advantages of birth or position to induce the old man to consent to a union which must involve his niece and ward in the strugglings and difficulties of a young and nearly friendless artist. He was, therefore, to wait until time had furnished him with opportunity, and accident with success; and then, if his labors were found sufficiently lucrative, it was to be hoped that his proposals might at least be listened to by her jealous guardian. Months passed away, and, cheered by the smiles of the little Rose, Schalken's labors were redoubled, and with such effect and improvement as reasonably to promise the realization of his hopes, and no contemptible eminence in his art, before many years should have elapsed.

The even course of this cheering prosperity was, however, destined to experience a sudden and formidable interruption, and that, too, in a manner so strange and mysterious as to baffle all investigation, and throw upon the events themselves a shadow of almost supernatural horror.

Schalken had one evening remained in the master's studio considerably longer than his more volatile companions, who had gladly availed themselves of the excuse which the dusk of evening afforded, to withdraw from their several tasks, in order to finish a day of labor in the jollity and conviviality of the tavern.

But Schalken worked for improvement, or rather for love. Besides, he was now engaged merely in sketching a design, an operation which, unlike that of coloring, might be continued as long as there was light sufficient to distinguish between canvas and charcoal. He had not then, nor, indeed, until long after, discovered the peculiar powers of his pencil, and he was engaged in composing a group of extremely roguish-looking and grotesque imps and demons, who were inflicting various ingenious torments upon a perspiring and pot-bellied St. Anthony, who reclined in the midst of them, apparently in the last stage of drunkenness.

The young artist, however, though incapable of executing, or even of appreciating, anything of true sublimity, had nevertheless discernment enough to prevent his being by any means satisfied with his work; and many were the patient erasures and corrections which the limbs and features of saint and devil underwent, yet all without producing in their new arrangement anything of improvement or increased effect.

The large, old-fashioned room was silent, and, with the exception of himself, quite deserted by its usual inmates. An hour had passed — nearly two — without any improved result. Daylight had already declined, and twilight was fast giving way to the darkness of night. The patience of the young man was exhausted, and he stood before his unfinished production, absorbed in no very pleasing ruminations, one hand buried in the folds of his long dark hair, and the other holding the piece of charcoal which had so ill executed its office, and which he now rubbed, without much regard to the sable streaks which it produced, with irritable pressure upon his ample Flemish inexpressibles.

"Pshaw!" said the young man aloud, "would that picture, devils, saint, and all, were where they should be — in hell!"

A short, sudden laugh, uttered startlingly close to his ear, instantly responded to the ejaculation.

The artist turned sharply round, and now for the first time became aware that his labors had been over-looked by a stranger.

Within about a yard and a half, and rather behind him, there stood what was, or appeared to be, the figure of an elderly man: he wore a short cloak, and broad-brimmed hat with a conical crown, and in his hand, which was protected with a heavy, gauntlet-shaped glove, he carried a long ebony walking-stick, sur-mounted with what appeared, as it glittered dimly in the twilight, to be a massive head of gold, and upon his breast, through the folds of the cloak, there shone what appeared to be the links of a rich chain of the same metal.

The room was so obscure that nothing further of the appearance of the figure could be ascertained, and the face was altogether overshadowed by the heavy flap of the beaver which overhung it, so that not a feature could be discerned. A quantity of dark hair escaped from beneath this somber hat, a circumstance which, connected with the firm, upright carriage of the in-truder, proved that his years could not yet exceed threescore or thereabouts.

There was an air of gravity and importance about the garb of this person, and something indescribably odd, I might say awful, in the perfect, stone-like mov-elessness of the figure, that effectually checked the testy comment which had at once risen to the lips of the irritated artist. He therefore, as soon as he had suffi-ciently recovered the surprise, asked the stranger, civilly, to be seated, and desired to know if he had any message to leave for his master.

"Tell Gerard Douw," said the unknown, without altering his attitude in the smallest degree, "that Mynher Vanderhauseny of Rotterdam, desires to speak with him tomorrow evening at this hour, and, if he please, in this room, upon matters of weight — that is all. Good-night."

The stranger, having finished this message, turned abruptly, and, with a quick but silent step, quitted the room, before Schalken had time to say a word in reply.

The young man felt a curiosity to see in what direction the burgher of Rotterdam would turn on quitting the studio, and for that purpose he went directly to the window which commanded the door.

A lobby of considerable extent intervened between the inner door of the painter's room and the street entrance, so that Schalken occupied the post of observation before the old man could possibly have reached the street.

He watched in vain, however. There was no other mode of exit.

Had the old man vanished, or was he lurking about the recesses of the lobby for some bad purpose? This last suggestion filled the mind of Schalken with a vague horror, which was so unaccountably intense as to make him alike afraid to remain in the room alone and reluctant to pass through the lobby.

However, with an effort which appeared very disproportioned to the occasion, he summoned resolution to leave the room, and, having double-locked the door and thrust the key in his pocket, without looking to the right or left, he traversed the passage which had so recently, perhaps still, contained the person of his mysterious visitant, scarcely venturing to breathe till he had arrived in the open street.

"Mynher Vanderhausen," said Gerard Douw within

himself, as the appointed hour approached, "Mynher Vanderhausen of Rotterdam! I never heard of the man till yesterday. What can he want of me? A portrait, perhaps, to be painted; or a younger son or a poor relation to be apprenticed; or a collection to be valued; or — pshaw I there's no one in Rotterdam to leave me a legacy. Well, whatever the business may be, we shall soon know it all."

It was now the close of day, and every easel, except that of Schalken, was deserted. Gerard Douw was pacing the apartment with the restless step of impatient expectation, every now and then humming a passage from a piece of music which he was himself composing; for, though no great proficient, he admired the art; sometimes pausing to glance over the work of one of his absent pupils, but more frequently placing himself at the window, from whence he might observe the passengers who threaded the obscure by-street in which his studio was placed.

"Said you not, Godfrey," exclaimed Douw, after a long and fruitless gaze from his post of observation, and turning to Schalken — "said you not the hour of appointment was at about seven by the clock of the Stadhouse?"

"It had just told seven when I first saw him, sir," answered the student.

"The hour is close at hand, then," said the master, consulting a horologe as large and as round as a full-grown orange. "Mynher Vanderhausen, from Rotterdam — is it not so?"

"Such was the name."

"And an elderly man, richly clad?" continued Douw.

"As well as I might see," replied his pupil; "he could not be young, nor yet very old neither, and his dress was rich and grave, as might become a citizen of wealth and consideration."

At this moment the sonorous boom of the Stad-house clock told, stroke after stroke, the hour of seven; the eyes of both master and student were directed to the door; and it was not until the last peal of the old bell had ceased to vibrate, that Douw exclaimed:

"So, so; we shall have his worship presently — that is, if he means to keep his hour; if not, thou mayst wait for him, Godfrey, if you court the acquaintance of a capricious burgomaster. As for me, I think our old Leyden contains a sufficiency of such commodities, without an importation from Rotterdam."

Schalken laughed, as in duty bound; and after a pause of some minutes, Douw suddenly exclaimed:

"What if it should all prove a jest, a piece of mum-mery got up by Vankarp, or some such worthy! I wish you had run all risks, and cudgeled the old burgomas-ter, stadholder, or whatever else he may be, soundly. I would wager a dozen of Rhenish, his worship would have pleaded old acquaintance before the third appli-cation."

"Here he comes, sir," said Schalken, in a low admoni-tory tone; and instantly, upon turning towards the door, Gerard Douw observed the same figure which had, on the day before, so unexpectedly greeted the vision of his pupil Schalken.

There was something in the air and mien of the figure which at once satisfied the painter that there was no *mummery* in the case, and that he really stood in the presence of a man of worship; and so, without hesita-tion, he doffed his cap, and courteously saluting the stranger, requested him to be seated.

The visitor waved his hand slightly, as, if in acknow-ledgment of the courtesy, but remained standing.

"I have the honor to see Mynher Vanderhausen, of Rotterdam?" said Gerard Douw.

"The same," was the laconic reply of his visitant.

"I understand your worship desires to speak with me," continued Douw, "and I am here by appointment to wait your commands."

"Is that a man of trust?" said Vanderhausen, turning towards Schalken, who stood at a little distance behind his master.

"Certainly," replied Gerard.

"Then let him take this box and get the nearest jeweler or goldsmith to value its contents, and let him return hither with a certificate of the valuation."

At the same time he placed a small case, about nine inches square, in the hands of Gerard Douw, who was as much amazed at its weight as at the strange abruptness with which it was handed to him.

In accordance with the wishes of the stranger, he delivered it into the hands of Schalken, and repeating *his* directions, dispatched him upon the mission.

Schalken disposed his precious charge securely beneath the folds of his cloak, and rapidly traversing two or three narrow streets, he stopped at a corner house, the lower part of which was then occupied by the shop of a Jewish goldsmith.

Schalken entered the shop, and calling the little Hebrew into the obscurity of its back recesses, he proceeded to lay before him Vanderhausen's packet.

On being examined by the light of a lamp, it appeared entirely cased with lead, the outer surface of which was much scraped and soiled, and nearly white with age. This was with difficulty partially removed, and disclosed beneath a box of some dark and singularly hard wood; this, too, was forced, and after the removal of two or three folds of linen, its contents proved to be a mass of golden ingots, close packed, and, as the Jew declared, of the most perfect quality.

Every ingot underwent the scrutiny of the little Jew, who seemed to feel an epicurean delight in touching and testing these morsels of the glorious metal; and each one of them was replaced in the box with the exclamation:

"*Mein Gott,* how very perfect! not one grain of alloy — beautiful, beautiful!"

The task was at length finished, and the Jew certified under his hand the value of the ingots submitted to his examination to amount to many thousand rix-dollars.

With the desired document in his bosom, and the rich box of gold carefully pressed under his arm, and concealed by his cloak, he retraced his way, and entering the studio, found his master and the stranger in close conference.

Schalken had no sooner left the room, in order to execute the commission he had taken in charge, than Vanderhausen addressed Gerard Douw in the following terms:

"I may not tarry with you tonight more than a few minutes, and so I shall briefly tell you the matter upon which I come. You visited the town of Rotterdam some four months ago, and then I saw in the church of St. Lawrence your niece, Rose Velderkaust. I desire to marry her, and if I satisfy you as to the fact that I am very wealthy — more wealthy than any husband you could dream of for her — I expect that you will forward my views to the utmost of your authority. If you approve my proposal, you must close with it at once, for I cannot command time enough to wait for calculations and delays.

Gerard Douw was, perhaps, as much astonished as anyone could be by the very unexpected nature of Mynher Vanderhausen's communication; but he did not give vent to any unseemly expression of surprise, for besides the motives supplied by prudence and politeness, the painter experienced a kind of chill and

oppressive sensation, something like that which is supposed to affect a man who is placed unconsciously in
immediate contact with something to which he has a
natural antipathy — an undefined horror and dread
while standing in the presence of the eccentric stranger,
which made him very unwilling to say anything which
might reasonably prove offensive.

"I have no doubt," said Gerard, after two or three
prefatory hems, "that the connection which you propose would prove alike advantageous and honorable
to my niece; but you must be aware that she has a will
of her own, and may not acquiesce in what *we* may
design for her advantage."

"Do not seek to deceive me, Sir Painter," said Vanderhausen; "you are her guardian — she is your ward.
She is mine if *you* like to make her so."

The man of Rotterdam moved forward a little as he
spoke, and Gerard Douw, he scarce knew why, inwardly
prayed for the speedy return of Schalken.

"I desire," said the mysterious gentleman, "to place
in your hands at once an evidence of my wealth, and
a security for my liberal dealing with your niece. The
lad will return in a minute or two with a sum in value
five times the fortune which she has a right to expect
from a husband. This shall lie in your hands, together
with her dowry, and you may apply the united sum as
suits her interest best; it shall be all exclusively hers
while she lives. Is that liberal?"

Douw assented, and inwardly thought that fortune
had been extraordinarily kind to his niece. The
stranger, he thought, must be both wealthy and generous, and such an offer was not to be despised, though
made by a humorist, and one of no very prepossessing
presence.

Rose had no very high pretensions, for she was
almost without dowry; indeed, altogether so, excepting

so far as the deficiency had been supplied by the generosity of her uncle. Neither had she any right to raise any scruples against the match on the score of birth, for her own origin was by no means elevated; and as to other objections, Gerard resolved, and, indeed, by the usages of the time was warranted in resolving, not to listen to them for a moment.

"Sir," said he, addressing the stranger, "your offer is most liberal, and whatever hesitation I may feel in closing with it immediately, arises solely from my not having the honor of knowing anything of your family or station. Upon these points you can, of course, satisfy me without difficulty?"

"As to my respectability," said the stranger, dryly, "you must take that for granted at present; pester me with no inquiries; you can discover nothing more about me than I choose to make known. You shall have sufficient security for my respectability — my word, if you are honorable: if you are sordid, my gold."

"A testy old gentleman," thought Douw; "he must have his own way. But, all things considered, I am justified in giving my niece to him. Were she my own daughter, I would do the like by her. I will not pledge myself unnecessarily, however."

"You will not pledge yourself unnecessarily," said Vanderhausen, strangely uttering the very words which had just floated through the mind of his companion; "but you will do so if it *is* necessary, I presume; and I will show you that I consider it indispensable. If the gold I mean to leave in your hands satisfy you, and if you desire that my proposal shall not be at once withdrawn, you must, before I leave this room, write your name to this engagement."

Having thus spoken, he placed a paper in the hands of Gerard, the contents of which expressed an engagement entered into by Gerard Douw, to give to Wilken

Vanderhausen, of Rotterdam, in marriage, Rose Velderkaust, and so forth, within one week of the date hereof.

While the painter was employed in reading this covenant, Schalken, as we have stated, entered the studio, and having delivered the box and the valuation of the Jew into the hands of the stranger, he was about to retire, when Vanderhausen called to him to wait; and, presenting the case and the certificate to Gerard Douw, he waited in silence until he had satisfied himself by an inspection of both as to the value of the pledge left in his hands. At length he said:

"Are you content?"

The painter said he would fain have another day to consider.

"Not an hour," said the suitor, coolly.

"Well, then," said Douw, "I am content; it is a bargain."

"Then sign at once," said Vanderhausen; "I am weary."

At the same time he produced a small case of writing materials, and Gerard signed the important document.

"Let this youth witness the covenant," said the old man; and Godfrey Schalken unconsciously signed the instrument which bestowed upon another that hand which he had so long regarded as the object and reward of all his labors.

The compact being thus completed, the strange visitor folded up the paper, and stowed it safely in an inner pocket.

"I will visit you tomorrow night, at nine of the clock, at your house, Gerard Douw, and will see the subject of our contract. Farewell." And so saying, Wilken Vanderhausen moved stiffly, but rapidly out of the room.

Schalken, eager to resolve his doubts, had placed himself by the window in order to watch the street entrance; but the experiment served only to support his suspicions, for the old man did not issue from the door. This was very strange, very odd, very fearful. He and his master returned together, and talked but little on the way, for each had his own subjects of reflection, of anxiety, and of hope.

Schalken, however, did not know the ruin which threatened his cherished schemes.

Gerard Douw knew nothing of the attachment which had sprung up between his pupil and his niece; and even if he had, it is doubtful whether he would have regarded its existence as any serious obstruction to the wishes of Mynher Vanderhausen.

Marriages were then and there matters of traffic and calculation; and it would have appeared as absurd in the eyes of the guardian to make a mutual attachment an essential element in a contract of marriage, as it would have been to draw up his bonds and receipts in the language of chivalrous romance.

The painter, however, did not communicate to his niece the important step which he had taken in her behalf, and his resolution arose not from any anticipation of opposition on her part, but solely from a ludicrous consciousness that if his ward were, as she very naturally might do, to ask him to describe the appearance of the bridegroom whom he destined for her, he would be forced to confess that he had not seen his face, and, if called upon, would find it impossible to identify him.

Upon the next day, Gerard Douw having dined, called his niece to him, and having scanned her person with an air of satisfaction, he took her hand, and looking upon her pretty, innocent face with a smile of kindness, he said:

"Rose, my girl, that face of yours will make your fortune." Rose blushed and smiled. "Such faces and such tempers seldom go together, and, when they do, the compound is a love-potion which few heads or hearts can resist. Trust me, thou wilt soon be a bride, girl. But this is trifling, and I am pressed for time, so make ready the large room by eight o'clock tonight, and give directions for supper at nine. I expect a friend tonight; and observe me, child, do thou trick thyself out handsomely. I would not have him think us poor or sluttish."

With these words he left the chamber, and took his way to the room to which we have already had occasion to introduce our readers — that in which his pupils worked.

When the evening closed in, Gerard called Schalken, who was about to take his departure to his obscure and comfortless lodgings, and asked him to come home and sup with Rose and Vanderhausen.

The invitation was of course accepted, and Gerard Douw and his pupil soon found themselves in the handsome and somewhat antique-looking room which had been prepared for the reception of the stranger.

A cheerful wood-fire blazed in the capacious hearth; a little at one side an old-fashioned table, with richly-carved legs, was placed — destined, no doubt, to receive the supper, for which preparations were going forward; and ranged with exact regularity, stood the tall-backed chairs, whose ungracefulness was more than counter-balanced by their comfort.

The little party, consisting of Rose, her uncle, and the artist, awaited the arrival of the expected visitor with considerable impatience.

Nine o'clock at length came, and with it a summons at the street-door, which, being speedily answered, was followed by a slow and emphatic tread upon the stair-case; the steps moved heavily across the lobby, the door of the room in which the party which we have described were assembled slowly opened, and there entered a figure which startled, almost appalled, the phlegmatic Dutchmen, and nearly made Rose scream with affright; it was the form, and arrayed in the garb, of Mynher Vanderhausen; the air, the gait, the height was the same, but the features had never been seen by any of the party before.

The stranger stopped at the door of the room, and displayed his form and face completely. He wore a dark-colored cloth cloak, which was short and full, not falling quite to the knees; his legs were cased in dark purple silk stockings, and his shoes were adorned with roses of the same color. The opening of the cloak in front showed the under-suit to consist of some very dark, perhaps sable material, and his hands were enclosed in a pair of heavy leather gloves which ran up considerably above the wrist, in the manner of a gauntlet. In one hand he carried his walking-stick and his hat, which he had removed, and the other hung heavily by his side. A quantity of grizzled hair descended in long tresses from his head, and its folds rested upon the plaits of a stiff ruff, which effectually concealed his neck.

So far all was well; but the face! — all the flesh of the face was colored with the bluish leaden hue which is sometimes produced by the operation of metallic medicines administered in excessive quantities; the eyes were enormous, and the white appeared both above and below the iris, which gave to them an expression of insanity, which was heightened by their glassy fixedness; the nose was well enough, but the mouth was writhed considerably to one side, where it opened in order to give egress to two long, discolored fangs, which projected from the upper jaw, far below the lower lip; the hue of the lips themselves bore the usual relation to that of the face, and was consequently nearly black. The character of the face was malignant, even satanic, to the last degree; and, indeed, such a combination of horror could hardly be accounted for, except by supposing the corpse of some atrocious malefactor, which had long hung blackening upon the gibbet, to have at length become the habitation of a demon — the frightful sport of Satanic possession.

It was remarkable that the worshipful stranger suffered as little as possible of his flesh to appear, and that during his visit he did not once remove his gloves

Having stood for some moments at the door, Gerard Douw at length found breath and collectedness to bid him welcome, and, with a mute inclination of the head, the stranger stepped forward into the room.

There was something indescribably odd, even horrible, about all his motions, something indefinable, that was unnatural, un-human — it was as if the limbs were guided and directed by a spirit unused to the management of bodily machinery.

The stranger said hardly anything during his visit, which did not exceed half an hour; and the host himself could scarcely muster courage enough to utter the few necessary salutations and courtesies: and, indeed, such was the nervous terror which the presence of Vanderhausen inspired, that very little would have made all his entertainers fly bellowing from the room.

They had not so far lost all self-possession, however, as to fail to observe two strange peculiarities of their visitor.

During his stay he did not once suffer his eyelids to close, nor even to move in the slightest degree; and further, there was a death-like stillness in his whole person, owing to the total absence of the heaving motion of the chest, caused by the process of respiration.

These two peculiarities, though when told they may

appear trifling, produced a very striking and unpleasant effect when seen and observed. Vanderhausen at length relieved the painter of Leyden of his inauspicious presence; and with no small gratification the little party heard the street-door close after him.

"Dear uncle," said Rose, "what a frightful man! I would not see him again for the wealth of the States!"

"Tush, foolish girl!" said Douw, whose sensations were anything but comfortable. "A man may be as ugly as the devil, and yet if his heart and actions are good, he is worth all the pretty-faced, perfumed puppies that walk the Mall. Rose, my girl, it is very true he has not thy pretty face, but I know him to be wealthy and liberal; and were he ten times more ugly —"

"Which is inconceivable," observed Rose.

"These two virtues would be sufficient," continued her uncle, "to counterbalance all his deformity; and if not of power sufficient actually to alter the shape of the features, at least of efficacy enough to prevent one thinking them amiss."

"Do you know, uncle," said Rose, "when I saw him standing at the door, I could not get it out of my head that I saw the old, painted, wooden figure that used to frighten me so much in the church of St. Laurence of Rotterdam."

Gerard laughed, though he could not help inwardly acknowledging the justness of the comparison. He was resolved, however, as far as he could, to check his niece's inclination to ridicule the ugliness of her intended bridegroom, although he was not a little pleased to observe that she appeared totally exempt from that mysterious dread of the stranger which, he could not disguise it from himself, considerably affected him, as also his pupil Godfrey Schalken.

Early on the next day there arrived, from various quarters of the town, rich presents of silks, velvets, jewelry, and so forth, for Rose; and also a packet directed to Gerard Douw, which, on being opened, was found to contain a contract of marriage, formally drawn up, between Wilken Vanderhausen of the Boom-quay, in Rotterdam, and Rose Velderkaust of Leyden, niece to Gerard Douw, master in the art of painting, also of the same city; and containing engagements on the part of Vanderhausen to make settlements upon his bride, far more splendid than he had before led her guardian to believe likely, and which were to be secured to her use in the most unexceptionable manner possible — the money being placed in the hands of Gerard Douw himself.

I have no sentimental scenes to describe, no cruelty of guardians, or magnanimity of wards, or agonies of lovers. The record I have to make is one of sordidness, levity, and interest. In less than a week after the first interview which we have just described, the contract of marriage was fulfilled, and Schalken saw the prize which he would have risked anything to secure, carried off triumphantly by his formidable rival.

For two or three days he absented himself from the school; he then returned and worked, if with less cheerfulness, with far more dogged resolution than before; the dream of love had given place to that of ambition.

Months passed away, and, contrary to his expectation, and, indeed, to the direct promise of the parties, Gerard Douw heard nothing of his niece, or her worshipful spouse. The interest of the money, which was to have been demanded in quarterly sums, lay unclaimed in his hands. He began to grow extremely uneasy.

Mynher Vanderhausen's direction in Rotterdam he was fully possessed of. After some irresolution he finally determined to journey thither — a trifling undertaking, and easily accomplished — and thus to satisfy himself of the safety and comfort of his ward, for whom he entertained an honest and strong affection.

His search was in vain, however. No one in Rotterdam had ever heard of Mynher Vanderhausen.

Gerard Douw left not a house in the Boom-quay untried; but all in vain. No one could give him any information whatever touching the object of his inquiry; and he was obliged to return to Leyden, nothing wiser than when he had left it.

On his arrival he hastened to the establishment from which Vanderhausen had hired the lumbering though, considering the times, most luxurious vehicle which the bridal party had employed to convey them to Rotterdam. From the driver of this machine he learned, that having proceeded by slow stages, they had late in the evening approached Rotterdam; but that before they entered the city, and while yet nearly a mile from it, a small party of men, soberly clad, and after the old fashion, with peaked beards and moustaches, standing in the center of the road, obstructed the further progress of the carriage. The driver reined in his horses, much fearing, from the obscurity of the hour, and the loneliness of the road, that some mischief was intended.

His fears were, however, somewhat allayed by his observing that these strange men carried a large litter, of an antique shape, and which they immediately set down upon the pavement, whereupon the bridegroom, having opened the coach-door from within, descended, and having assisted his bride to do likewise, led her, weeping bitterly and wringing her hands, to the litter, which they both entered. It was then raised by the men who surrounded it, and speedily carried towards the city, and before it had proceeded many yards the darkness concealed it from the view of the Dutch charioteer.

In the inside of the vehicle he found a purse, whose contents more than thrice paid the hire of the carriage and man. He saw and could tell nothing more of Mynher Vanderhausen and his beautiful lady. This mystery was a source of deep anxiety and almost of grief to Gerard Douw.

There was evidently fraud in the dealing of Vanderhausen with him, though for what purpose committed he could not imagine. He greatly doubted how far it was possible for a man possessing in his countenance so strong an evidence of the presence of the most demoniac feelings, to be in reality anything but a villain; and every day that passed without his hearing from or of his niece, instead of inducing him to forget his fears, on the contrary tended more and more to exasperate them.

The loss of his niece's cheerful society tended also to depress his spirits; and in order to dispel this despondency, which often crept upon his mind after his daily employment was over, he was wont frequently to prevail upon Schalken to accompany him home, and by his presence to dispel, in some degree, the gloom of his otherwise solitary supper.

One evening, the painter and his pupil were sitting by the fire, having accomplished a comfortable supper, and had yielded to that silent pensiveness sometimes induced by the process of digestion, when their reflections were disturbed by a loud sound at the street-door, as if occasioned by some person rushing forcibly and repeatedly against it. A domestic had run without delay to ascertain the cause of the disturbance, and they heard him twice or thrice interrogate the applicant for admission, but without producing an answer or any cessation of the sounds.

They heard him then open the hall-door, and immediately there followed a light and rapid tread upon the staircase. Schalken laid his hand on his sword, and advanced towards the door. It opened before he reached it, and Rose rushed into the room. She looked wild and haggard, and pale with exhaustion and terror; but her dress surprised them as much even as her unexpected appearance. It consisted of a kind of white woolen wrapper, made close about the neck, and descending to the very ground. It was much deranged and travel-soiled. The poor creature had hardly entered the chamber when she fell senseless on the floor. With some difficulty they succeeded in reviving her, and on recovering her senses she instantly exclaimed, in a tone of eager, terrified impatience:

"Wine, wine, quickly, or I'm lost!"

Much alarmed at the strange agitation in which the call was made, they at once administered to her wishes, and she drank some wine with a haste and eagerness which surprised them. She had hardly swallowed it, when she exclaimed, with the same urgency:

"Food, food, at once, or I perish!"

A considerable fragment of a roast joint was upon the table, and Schalken immediately proceeded to cut some, but he was anticipated; for no sooner had she become aware of its presence than she darted at it with the rapacity of a vulture, and, seizing it in her hands she tore off the flesh with her teeth and swallowed it.

When the paroxysm of hunger had been a little appeased, she appeared suddenly to become aware how strange her conduct had been, or it may have been that other more agitating thoughts recurred to her mind, for she began to weep bitterly and to wring her hands.

"Oh! send for a minister of God," said she; "I am not safe till he comes; send for him speedily."

Gerard Douw dispatched a messenger instantly, and prevailed on his niece to allow him to surrender his bedchamber to her use; he also persuaded her to retire to it at once and to rest; her consent was extorted upon the condition that they would not leave her for a moment.

"Oh that the holy man were here!" she said; "he can deliver me. The dead and the living can never be one — God has forbidden it."

With these mysterious words she surrendered herself to their guidance, and they proceeded to the chamber which Gerard Douw had assigned to her use.

"Do not — do not leave me for a moment," said she. "I am lost forever if you do."

Gerard Douw's chamber was approached through a spacious apartment, which they were now about to enter. Gerard Douw and Schalken each carried a was candle, so that a sufficient degree of light was cast upon all surrounding objects. They were now entering the large chamber, which, as I have said, communicated with Douw's apartment, when Rose suddenly stopped, and, in a whisper which seemed to thrill with horror, she said:

"O God! he is here — he is here! See, see — there he goes!"

She pointed towards the door of the inner room, and Schalken thought he saw a shadowy and ill-defined form gliding into that apartment. He drew his sword, and raising the candle so as to throw its light with increased distinctness upon the objects in the room, he entered the chamber into which the shadow had glided. No figure was there — nothing but the furniture which belonged to the room, and yet he could not be deceived as to the fact that something had moved before them into the chamber.

A sickening dread came upon him, and the cold perspiration broke out in heavy drops upon his forehead; nor was he more composed when he heard the increased urgency, the agony of entreaty, with which

Rose implored them not to leave her for a moment.

"I saw him," said she. "He's here! I cannot be deceived — I know him. He's by me — he's with me — he's in the room. Then, for God's sake, as you would save, do not stir from beside me!"

They at length prevailed upon her to lie down upon the bed, where she continued to urge them to stay by her. She frequently uttered incoherent sentences, repeating again and again, "The dead and the living cannot be one — God has forbidden it!" and then again, "Rest to the wakeful — sleep to the sleep-walkers."

These and such mysterious and broken sentences she continued to utter until the clergyman arrived.

Gerard Douw began to fear, naturally enough, that the poor girl, owing to terror or ill-treatment, had become deranged; and he half suspected, by the suddenness of her appearance, and the unseasonableness of the hour, and, above all, from the wildness and terror of her manner, that she had made her escape from some place of confinement for lunatics, and was in immediate fear of pursuit. He resolved to summon medical advice as soon as the mind of his niece had been in some measure set at rest by the offices of the clergyman whose attendance she had so earnestly desired; and until this object had been attained, he did not venture to put any questions to her, which might possibly, by reviving painful or horrible recollections, increase her agitation.

The clergyman soon arrived — a man of ascetic countenance and venerable age — one whom Gerard Douw respected much, forasmuch as he was a veteran polemic, though one, perhaps, more dreaded as a combatant than beloved as a Christian — of pure morality, subtle brain, and frozen heart. He entered the chamber which communicated with that in which Rose reclined, and immediately on his arrival she requested him to pray for her, as for one who lay in the hands of Satan, and who could hope for deliverance — only from heaven.

That our readers may distinctly understand all the circumstances of the event which we are about imperfectly to describe, it is necessary to state the relative position of the parties who were engaged in it. The old clergyman and Schalken were in the anteroom of which we have already spoken; Rose lay in the inner chamber, the door of which was open; and by the side of the bed, at her urgent desire, stood her guardian; a candle burned in the bed-chamber, and three were lighted in the outer apartment

The old man now cleared his voice, as if about to commence; but before he had time to begin, a sudden gust of air blew out the candle which served to illuminate the room in which the poor girl lay, and she, with hurried alarm, exclaimed:

"Godfrey, bring in another candle; the darkness is unsafe."

Gerard Douw, forgetting for the moment her repeated injunctions in the immediate impulse, stepped from the bedchamber into the other, in order to supply what she desired.

"O God I do not go, dear uncle!" shrieked the unhappy girl; and at the same time she sprang from the bed and darted after him, in order, by her grasp, to detain him.

But the warning came too late, for scarcely had he passed the threshold, and hardly had his niece had time to utter the startling exclamation, when the door which divided the two rooms closed violently after him, as if swung to by a strong blast of wind.

Schalken and he both rushed to the door, but their united and desperate efforts could not avail so much as to shake it.

Shriek after shriek burst from the inner chamber, with all the piercing loudness of despairing terror. Schalken and Douw applied every energy and strained every nerve to force open the door; but all in vain.

There was no sound of struggling from within, but the screams seemed to increase in loudness, and at the same time they heard the bolts of the latticed window withdrawn, and the window itself grated upon the sill as if thrown open.

One *last* shriek, so long and piercing and agonized as to be scarcely human, swelled from the room, and suddenly there followed a death-like silence.

A light step was heard crossing the floor, as if from the bed to the window; and almost at the same instant the door gave way, and, yielding to the pressure of the external applicants, they were nearly precipitated into the room. It was empty. The window was open, and Schalken sprang to a chair and gazed out upon the street and canal below. He saw no form, but he beheld, or thought he beheld, the waters of the broad canal beneath settling ring after ring in heavy circular ripples, as if a moment before disturbed by the immersion of some large and heavy mass.

No trace of Rose was ever after discovered, nor was anything certain respecting her mysterious wooer detected or even suspected; no clue whereby to trace the intricacies of the labyrinth and to arrive at a distinct conclusion was to be found. But an incident occurred, which, though it will not be received by our rational readers as at all approaching to evidence upon the matter, nevertheless produced a strong and a lasting impression upon the mind of Schalken.

Many years after the events which we have detailed, Schalken, then remotely situated, received an intimation of his father's death, and of his intended burial upon a fixed day in the church of Rotterdam. It was necessary that a very considerable journey should be performed by the funeral procession, which, as it will readily be believed, was not very numerously attended. Schalken with difficulty arrived in Rotterdam late in the day upon which the funeral was appointed to take place. The procession had not then arrived. Evening closed in, and still it did not appear.

Schalken strolled down to the church — be found it open — notice of the arrival of the funeral had been given, and the vault in which the body was to be laid had been opened. The official who corresponds to our sexton, on seeing a well-dressed gentleman, whose object was to attend the expected funeral, pacing the aisle of the church, hospitably invited him to share with him the comforts of a blazing wood fire, which, as was his custom in winter time upon such occasions, he had kindled on the hearth of a chamber which communicated, by a flight of steps, with the vault below.

In this chamber Schalken and his entertainer seated themselves, and the sexton, after some fruitless attempts to engage his guest in conversation, was obliged to apply himself to his tobacco-pipe and can to solace his solitude.

In spite of his grief and cares, the fatigues of a rapid journey of nearly forty hours gradually overcame the mind and body of Godfrey Schalken, and he sank into a deep sleep, from which he was awakened by some one shaking him gently by the shoulder. He first thought that the old sexton had called him, but *he* was no longer in the room.

He roused himself, and as soon as he could clearly see what was around him, he perceived a female form, clothed in a kind of light robe of muslin, part of which was so disposed as to act as a veil, and in her hand she carried a lamp. She was moving rather away from him, and towards the flight of steps which conducted towards the vaults.

Schalken felt a vague alarm at the sight of this figure, and at the same time an irresistible impulse to follow its guidance. He followed it towards the vaults, but when it reached the head of the stairs, he paused; the figure paused also, and, turning gently round, displayed, by the light of the lamp it carried, the face and features of his first love, Rose Velderkaust. There was nothing horrible, or even sad, in the countenance. On the contrary, it wore the same arch smile which used to enchant the artist long before in his happy days.

A feeling of awe and of interest, too intense to be resisted, prompted him to follow the specter, if specter it were. She descended the stairs — he followed; and, turning to the left, through a narrow passage, she led him, to his infinite surprise, into what appeared to be an old-fashioned Dutch apartment, such as the pictures of Gerard Douw have served to immortalize.

Abundance of costly antique furniture was disposed about the room, and in one corner stood a four-post bed, with heavy black-cloth curtains around it; the figure frequently turned towards him with the same arch smile; and when she came to the side of the bed, she drew the curtains, and by the light of the lamp which she held towards its contents, she disclosed to the horror-stricken painter, sitting bolt upright in the bed, the livid and demoniac form of Vanderhausen. Schalken had hardly seen him when he fell senseless upon the floor, where he lay until discovered, on the next morning, by persons employed in closing the passages into the vaults. He was lying in a cell of considerable size, which had not been disturbed for a long time, and he had fallen beside a large coffin which was supported upon small stone pillars, a security against the attacks of vermin.

To his dying day Schalken was satisfied of the reality

of the vision which he had witnessed, and he has left behind him a curious evidence of the impression which it wrought upon his fancy, in a painting executed shortly after the event we have narrated, and which is valuable as exhibiting not only the peculiarities which have made Schalken's pictures sought after, but even more so as presenting a portrait, as close and faithful as one taken from memory can be, of his early love, Rose Velderkaust, whose mysterious fate must ever remain matter of speculation.

The picture represents a chamber of antique masonry, such as might be found in most old cathedrals, and is lighted faintly by a lamp carried in the hand of a female figure, such as we have above attempted to describe; and in the background, and to the left of him who examines the painting, there stands the form of a man apparently aroused from sleep, and by his attitude, his hand being laid upon his sword, exhibiting considerable alarm: this last figure is illuminated only by the expiring glare of a wood or charcoal fire.

The whole production exhibits a beautiful specimen of that artful and singular distribution of light and shade which has rendered the name of Schalken immortal among the artists of his country. This tale is traditionary, and the reader will easily perceive, by our studiously omitting to heighten many points of the narrative, when a little additional coloring might have added effect to the recital, that we have desired to lay before him, not a figment of the brain, but a curious tradition connected with, and belonging to, the biography of a famous artist.

Scraps of Hibernian Ballads

Being an Eighth Extract from the Legacy of the late Francis Purcell, P.P. of Drumcoolagh

I have observed, my dear friend, among other grievous misconceptions current among men otherwise well-informed, and which tend to degrade the pretensions of my native land, an impression that there exists no such thing as indigenous modern Irish composition deserving the name of poetry — a belief which has been thoughtlessly sustained and confirmed by the unconscionable literary perverseness of Irishmen themselves, who have preferred the easy task of concocting humorous extravaganzas, which caricature with merciless exaggeration the pedantry, bombast, and blunders incident to the lowest order of Hibernian ballads, to the more pleasurable and patriotic duty of collecting together the many, many specimens of genuine poetic feeling, which have grown up, like its wild flowers, from the warm though neglected soil of Ireland.

In fact, the productions which have long been regarded as pure samples of Irish poetic composition, such as "The Groves of Blarney," and "The Wedding of Ballyporeen," "Ally Croker," etc., etc., are altogether spurious, and as much like the thing they call themselves "as I to Hercules."

There are to be sure in Ireland, as in all countries, poems which deserve to be laughed at. The native productions of which I speak, frequently abound in absurdities — absurdities which are often, too, provokingly mixed up with what is beautiful; but I strongly and absolutely deny that the prevailing or even the usual character of Irish poetry is that of comicality. No country, no time, is devoid of real poetry, or something approaching to it; and surely it were a strange thing if Ireland, abounding as she does from shore to shore with all that is beautiful, and grand, and savage in scenery, and filled with wild recollections, vivid passions, warm affections, and keen sorrow, could find no language to speak withal, but that of mummery and jest. No, her language is imperfect, but there is strength in its rudeness, and beauty in its wildness; and, above all, strong feeling flows through it, like fresh fountains in rugged caverns.

And yet I will not say that the language of genuine indigenous Irish composition is always vulgar and uncouth: on the contrary, I am in possession of some specimens, though by no means of the highest order as to poetic merit, which do not possess throughout a single peculiarity of diction. The lines which I now proceed to lay before you, by way of illustration, are from the pen of an unfortunate young man, of very humble birth, whose early hopes were crossed by the untimely death of her whom he loved. He was a self-educated man, and in afterlife rose to high distinctions in the Church to which he devoted himself — an act which proves the sincerity of spirit with which these verses were written.

"When moonlight falls on wave and wimple,
And silvers every circling dimple,
That onward, onward sails:
When fragrant hawthorns wild and simple
Lend perfume to the gales,
And the pale moon in heaven abiding,
O'er midnight mists and mountains riding,
Shines on the river, smoothly gliding
Through quiet dales,

"I wander there in solitude,
Charmed by the chiming music rude
Of streams that fret and flow.
For by that eddying stream *she* stood,
On such a night I trow:
For *her* the thorn its breath was lending,
On this same tide *her* eye was bending,
And with its voice *her* voice was blending
Long, long ago.

Wild stream! I walk by thee once more,
I see thy hawthorns dim and hoar,
I hear thy waters moan,
And night-winds sigh from shore to shore,
With hushed and hollow tone;
But breezes on their light way winging,
And all thy waters heedless singing,
No more to me are gladness bringing —
I am alone.

"Years after years, their swift way keeping,
Like sere leaves down thy current sweeping,
Are lost for aye, and sped —
And Death the wintry soil is heaping
As fast as flowers are shed.
And she who wandered by my side,
And breathed enchantment o'er thy tide,
That makes thee still my friend and guide —
And she is dead."

These lines I have transcribed in order to prove a point which I have heard denied, namely, that an Irish peasant — for their author was no more — may write at least correctly in the matter of measure, language, and rhyme; and I shall add several extracts in further illustration of the same fact, a fact whose assertion, it must be allowed, may appear somewhat paradoxical even to those who are acquainted, though superficially, with Hibernian composition. The rhymes are, it must be granted, in the generality of such productions, very latitudinarian indeed, and as a veteran votary of the muse once assured me, depend wholly upon the *wowls* (vowels), as may be seen in the following stanza of the famous "Shanavan Voicth."

"'What'll we have for supper?'
Says my Shanavan Voicth;
'We'll have turkeys and roast *beef*,
And we'll eat it very *sweet*,
And then we'll take a *sleep*,'
Says my Shanavan Voicth."

But I am desirous of showing you that, although barbarisms may and do exist in our native ballads, there are still to be found exceptions which furnish examples of strict correctness in rhyme and meter. Whether they be one whit the better for this I have my doubts. In order to establish my position, I subjoin a portion of a ballad by one Michael Finley, of whom more anon. The *gentleman* spoken of in the song is Lord Edward Fitzgerald.

"The day that traitors sould him and inimies
                bought him,
The day that the red gold and red blood was paid —
Then the green turned pale and thrembled like the
                dead leaves in Autumn,
And the heart an' hope iv Ireland in the could grave
                was laid.

"The day I saw you first, with the sunshine fallin'
                round ye,
My heart fairly opened with the grandeur of the
                view:
For ten thousand Irish boys that day did surround
                ye,
An' I swore to stand by them till death, an' fight for
                you.

"Ye wor the bravest gentleman, an' the best that ever
                stood,
And your eyelid never thrembled for danger nor for
                dread,
An' nobleness was flowin' in each stream of your
                blood —
My bleasing on you night au' day, an' Glory be
                your bed.

"My black an' bitter curse on the head, an' heart,
                an' hand,
That plotted, wished, an' worked the fall of this

Irish hero bold;
God's curse upon the Irishman that sould his native
    land,
An' hell consume to dust the hand that held the
    thraitor's gold."

Such were the politics and poetry of Michael Finley,
in his day, perhaps, the most noted song-maker of his
country; but as genius is never without its eccentrici-
ties, Finley had his peculiarities, and among these,
perhaps the most amusing was his rooted aversion to
pen, ink, and paper, in perfect independence of which,
all his compositions were completed. It is impossible
to describe the jealousy with which he regarded the
presence of writing materials of any kind, and his ever
wakeful fears lest some literary pirate should transfer
his *oral* poetry to paper — fears which were not altogether without warrant, inasmuch as the recitation and
singing of these original pieces were to him a source
of wealth and importance. I recollect upon one occasion his detecting me in the very act of following his
recitation with my pencil and I shall not soon forget
his indignant scowl, as stopping abruptly in the midst
of a line, he sharply exclaimed:

"Is my *pome* a pigsty, or what, that you want a
surveyor's ground-plan of it?"

Owing to this absurd scruple, I have been obliged,
with one exception, that of the ballad of "Phaudhrig
Crohoore," to rest satisfied with such snatches and
fragments of his poetry as my memory could bear away
— a fact which must account for the mutilated state in
which I have been obliged to present the foregoing
specimen of his composition.

It was in vain for me to reason with this man of
meters upon the unreasonableness of this despotic and
exclusive assertion of copyright. I well remember his

answer to me when, among other arguments, I urged the advisability of some care for the permanence of his reputation, as a motive to induce him to consent to have his poems written down, and thus reduced to a palpable and enduring form.

"I often noticed," said he, "when a mist id be spreadin', a little brier to look as big, you'd think, as an oak tree; an' same way, in the dimness iv the nightfall, I often seen a man tremblin' and crassin' himself as if a sperit was before him, at the sight iv a small thorn bush, that he'd leap over with ase if the daylight and sunshine was in it. An' that's the rason why I think it id be better for the likes iv me to be remimbered in tradition than to be written in history.

Finley has now been dead nearly eleven years, and his fame has not prospered by the tactics which he pursued, for his reputation, so far from being magnified, has been wholly obliterated by the mists of obscurity.

With no small difficulty, and no inconsiderable maneuvering, I succeeded in procuring, at an expense of trouble and conscience which you will no doubt think but poorly rewarded, an accurate "report' of one of his most popular recitations. It celebrates one of the many daring exploits of the once famous Phaudhrig Crohoore (in prosaic English, Patrick Connor). I have witnessed powerful effects produced upon large assemblies by Finley's recitation of this poem which he was wont, upon pressing invitation, to deliver at weddings, wakes, and the like; of course the power of the narrative was greatly enhanced by the fact that many of his auditors had seen and well knew the chief actors in the drama.

Phaudhrig Crohoore

"Oh, Phaudhrig Crohoore was the broth of a boy,
And he stood six foot eight,
And his arm was as round as another man's thigh,
'Tis Phaudhrig was great, —
And his hair was as black as the shadows of night,
And hung over the scars left by many a fight;
And his voice, like the thunder, was deep, strong,
　　　　and loud,
And his eye like the lightnin' from under the cloud.
And all the girls liked him, for he could spake civil,
And sweet when he chose it, for he was the divil.
An' there wasn't a girl from thirty-five undher,
Divil a matter how crass, but he could come round
　　　her.
But of all the sweet girls that smiled on him, but one
Was the girl of his heart, an' he loved her alone.
An' warm as the sun, as the rock firm an' sure,
Was the love of the heart of Phaudhrig Crohoore;
An' he'd die for one smile from his Kathleen
　　　O'Brien,
For his love, like his hatred, was sthrong as the lion.

"But Michael O'Hanlon loved Kathleen as well
As he hated Crohoore — an' that same was like hell.
But O'Brien liked *him*, for they were the same par-
　　　ties,
The O'Briens, O'Hanlons, an' Murphys, and Car-
　　　tys —
An' they all went together an' hated Crohoore,
For it's many the batin' he gave them before;
An' O'Hanlon made up to O'Brien, an' says he:
'I'll marry your daughter, if you'll give her to me.'
And the match was made up, an' when Shrovetide

came on,
The company assimbled three hundred if one:
There was all the O'Hanlons, an' Murphys, an' Car-
       tys,
An' the young boys an' girls av all o' them parties;
An' the O'Briens, av coorse, gathered strong on day,
An' the pipers an' fiddlers were tearin' away;
There was roarin', an' jumpin', an' jiggin', an'
       flingin',
An' jokin', an' blessin', an' kissin', an' singin',
An' they wor all laughin' — why not, to be sure? —
How O'Hanlon came inside of Phaudhrig Crohoore.
An' they all talked an' laughed the length of the ta-
       ble,
Atin' an' dhrinkin' all while they wor able,
And with pipin' an' fiddlin' an' roarin' like tundher,
Your head you'd think fairly was splittin' asundher;
And the priest called out, 'Silence, ye blackguards,
       agin!'
An' he took up his prayer-book, just goin' to begin,
An' they all held their tongues from their funnin'
       and bawlin',
So silent you'd notice the smallest pin fallin';
An' the priest was just beg'nin' to read, whin the
       door
Sprung back to the wall, and in walked Crohoore —
Oh! Phaudhrig Crohoore was the broth of a boy,
Ant he stood six foot eight,
An' his arm was as round as another man's thigh,
'Tis Phaudhrig was great —
An' he walked slowly up, watched by many a bright
       eye,
As a black cloud moves on through the stars of the
       sky,
An' none sthrove to stop him, for Phaudhrig was
       great,

Till he stood all alone, just apposit the sate
Where O'Hanlon and Kathleen, his beautiful bride,
Were sitting so illigant out side by side;
An' he gave her one look that her heart almost
              broke,
An' he turned to O'Brien, her father, and spoke,
An' his voice, like the thunder, was deep, sthrong,
              and loud,
An' his eye shone like lightnin' from under the
              cloud:
'I didn't come here like a tame, crawlin' mouse,
But I stand like a man in my inimy's house;
In the field, on the road, Phaudhrig never knew fear,
Of his foemen, an' God knows he scorns it here;
So lave me at aise, for three minutes or four,
To spake to the girl I'll never see more.'
An' to Kathleen he turned, and his voice changed
              its tone,
For he thought of the days when he called her his
              own,
An' his eye blazed like lightnin' from under the
              cloud
On his false-hearted girl, reproachful and proud,
An' says he: 'Kathleen bawn, is it thrue what I hear,
That you marry of your free choice, without threat
              or fear?
If so, spake the word, an' I'll turn and depart,
Chated once, and once only by woman's false heart.'
Oh! sorrow and love made the poor girl dumb,
An' she thried hard to spake, but the words
              wouldn't come,
For the sound of his voice, as he stood there fornint
              her,
Wint could on her heart as the night wind in
              winther.
An' the tears in her blue eyes stood tremblin' to

flow,
And pale was her cheek as the moonshine on snow;
Then the heart of bould Phaudhrig swelled high in
     its place,
For he knew, by one look in that beautiful face,
That though sthrangers an' foemen their pledged
     hands might sever,
Her true heart was his, and his only, forever.
An' he lifted his voice, like the agle's hoarse call,
An' says Phaudhrig, 'She's mine still, in spite of yez
     all!'
Then up jumped O'Hanlon, an' a tall boy was he,
An' he looked on bould Phaudhrig as fierce as
     could be,
An' says he, 'By the hokey! before you go out,
Bould Phaudhrig Crohoore, you ,must fight for a
     bout.'
Then Phaudhrig made answer: 'I'll do my endeavor,'
An' with one blow he stretched bould O'Hanlon for-
     ever.
In his arms he took Kathleen, an' stepped to the
     door;
And he leaped on his horse, and flung her before;
An' they all were so bother'd, that not a man stirred
Till the galloping hoofs on the pavement were heard.
Then up they all started, like bees in the swarm,
An' they riz a great shout, like the burst of a storm,
An' they roared, and they ran, and they shouted ga-
     lore;
But Kathleen and Phaudhrig they never saw more.
"But them days are gone by, an' he is no more;
An' the green-grass is growin' o'er Phaudhrig Cro-
     hoore,
For he couldn't be aisy or quiet at all;
As he lived a brave boy, he resolved so to fall.
And he took a good pike — for Phaudhrig was

        great —
And he fought, and he died in the year ninety-eight.
An' the day that Crohoore in the green field was
            killed,
A sthrong boy was sthretched, and a sthrong heart
            was stilled."

It is due to the memory of Finley to say that the foregoing ballad. though bearing throughout a strong resemblance to Sir Walter Scott's "Lochinvar," was nevertheless composed long before that spirited production had seen the light.

Printed in the United States
R12030210113701PG7470D001B-2